DARK PATH

A BODHI KING NOVEL

MELISSA F. MILLER

BROWN STREET BOOKS

Published by Brown Street Books.

Brown Street Books ISBN: 978-1-940759-30-2

ALSO BY MELISSA F. MILLER

Chilling Effect

Calculated Risk

The Bodhi King Novels

Dark Path

Lonely Path

Hidden Path

The We Sisters Three Romantic Comedic Mysteries

Rosemary's Gravy

Sage of Innocence

Thyme to Live

Lost and Gowned

CHAPTER ONE

*A faithful man will abound with
blessings,
but he who hastens to be rich will not
go unpunished.*

PROVERBS 28:20

*Whatever precious jewel there is in the
heavenly worlds, there is nothing
comparable to one who is
Awakened.*

THE BUDDHA, SUTTA NIPATA

"Do you love the Lord?"

The assembled group roared a hearty 'yes.'

"With all your heart?"

Another affirmation rang through the auditorium.

Pastor Bryce Scott waited until the echo died down. Then he raised his arms and searched the upturned faces at the edge of the elevated stage. "No, you do not. And do you know how I know?"

The room fell silent.

Bryce paced from one end of the platform to the other, as if he were a caged panther or a particularly nervous TED Talk speaker. The spotlights barely registered. He'd grown accustomed to their heat and brightness. He was full of the Spirit.

He continued, his voice taking on the cadence he used in his sermons, "Because if you love God, God will love you. And when God loves you, He will reward you materially. Do you have a Mercedes? No, you do not. A gorgeous home? No. A boat? Why not? Because you have not blessed God, so God has not blessed you."

The air in the room grew heavy, still.

Bryce paused and allowed the uncomfortable silence to settle like a thick fog. Several members of the small, handpicked audience cast baleful, accusatory glances at one another. Several more studied their feet.

He waited, standing stock still in the middle of the stage, until the tension had grown, until it had neared a breaking point. Then he resumed his walking and talking.

"You have been anointed. Each of you—chosen. Now you must make a choice. Will you love God and reap His rewards? Will you answer the call? Or will you turn your back on God?"

Bryce's hands shot toward the ceiling again and, on cue, the music resumed its relentless beat. "You can be who you strive to be. Be what God wants for you! Be blessed in riches."

As the clapping and cheering crescendoed, he strode toward the wings. Offstage, he pulled the wireless mic from his head and thrust it into Becki's waiting hands. She handed him a chilled bottle of mineral water.

"How many still haven't signed their contracts?" He gulped the water while he waited for her answer. The cool liquid soothed his always-strained vocal cords.

Becki's blonde head bent over the clipboard and her eyes scanned the sheet. "Um, six. No, seven."

Bryce took another long drink of water.

Seven. Did these men not understand what he was offering them? Did they not want to live a life of abundance to glorify the Lord?

He shook his head at the thought. "Is the financial counselor in the vestibule?"

"Yes, sir. He brought his credit card reader, and we tested it. He's all set to take installment payments when they come out."

He flashed her his trademark white smile. "Good. Is my car out front?"

"Yes, sir. The driver called ahead to the captain. The yacht is ready, and the lobster and shrimp Mrs. Scott ordered from the fish market is below deck, on ice."

"Fresh?"

"They assured me it was caught today."

He rewarded her with another smile. "Very nice, Becki. You'll be blessed for your care. You're doing good and important work."

The young woman—barely out of her teens—flushed a deep pink and bobbed her head. "Thank you, Pastor Bryce."

He patted her arm then handed her the half-empty water bottle as he swept out of the satellite church. Before he could step into his waiting Mercedes, though, he was waylaid.

"Pastor Bryce, sir!" The man called out in an urgent way as he jogged behind him, through the doors.

Bryce turned and studied the jogging man's face as he approached the car. All his years in the pulpit had helped him develop a rock-solid memory for faces. His flock was too large now—well over ten thousand souls —for him to know each of his congregants individually, but he knew the name of every person he'd assembled for this talk.

Dark eyes behind thick glasses, olive skin, short-cropped black hair. Arthur Lopez. Single. He had been an information technology support specialist for Florida's Department of Education with a base salary of forty-nine thousand dollars a year. Arthur had been laid off back in the spring, but according to church records, he'd continued to meet his tithing targets without interruption.

"Arthur, is something wrong?" Bryce asked in a concerned voice, one hand on the frame of the car door.

"No, Pastor." Arthur came to a stop several feet away, panting slightly from the exertion. "Well, yes. I ..." His eyes dropped to the ground.

"What is it, son?"

"I don't have the money for the program. I mean,

not yet. I have ... circumstances. But I'll get it. Can I have a little more time?" Arthur dragged his eyes back up to Bryce's face with a pleading expression.

Bryce smiled broadly. "You don't honor God by acting poor, Arthur. You honor Him by living with abundance. You've been chosen for the Spread the Word Ministry because you're special. You need to believe it and invest in yourself."

"Yes, but, I need to secure financing."

"Didn't you see Robert in the lobby? He can put you on a plan."

"The interest rate ..." Arthur began in a meek voice.

"I have to run, Arthur. Let me tell you plainly—we can't hold your spot. So many faithful men and women would give anything to have a chance at what we're offering you. You need to make a decision to live abundantly."

"Of ... of course."

Bryce turned away from the stammering man and nodded to his driver, who'd been standing just outside the car, waiting. The driver opened the rear door, and Bryce slid onto the soft leather seat.

Arthur stood in the parking lot, shoulders slumping, and watched the car pull away.

Through the lightly tinted window, Bryce caught a

final glimpse of his tense, fretful expression as the car rounded the circular driveway. He promised himself to remember to pray for Arthur to find the strength of purpose to become a Spread the Word Ministerial Associate.

CHAPTER TWO

"**A**nother one?" Detective Felicia Williams asked. She hesitated in the doorway.

"Yes," Nurse Eduardo Martinez answered in a low, mournful voice. "I came in to take his vitals at the start of my shift, and there he was. Eyes open, a look of horror on his face, dead. Just like the others."

Felicia sighed. Carlos Garcia was the fourth person to die in this place in as many weeks. "How—" she began.

"Leesh, they're old. This *is* an assisted care facility."

She suddenly felt weary. Old enough to be a resident at Golden Shores instead of the officer charged with investigating cases that occurred within its confines.

"I know, Ed." She sighed. "But it's becoming a ... thing ... in the squad room. It makes me look bad, all these sudden, unexplained deaths."

He held her gaze for a long moment. She didn't glance away. They'd known each since they'd been in diapers. Two Conches who'd grown up on the same short street. They'd made their First Communion together. She'd copied off his test papers in Mr. Anderson's high school science classes.

She didn't have to tell him that, as the only female officer and the only Cuban-American in the homicide unit, she was held to a different, higher standard. As the only male nurse and the only Cuban-American working in the assisted care facility, Eduardo knew as well as she did how outsiders were treated. She needed to be better, to clear unclearable cases. Although she suspected Ed's female colleagues weren't quite as coarse as her coworkers were. The guys on the squad delighted in trying to break her.

Ed was still focused on the logic of it all. "How can they fault you? The medical examiner's office did the autopsies. They said the other three all died of natural causes, right?"

"Actually, they're putting unexplained causes on the death certificates. People don't like unexplained deaths. They seem to think deaths should have an explanation behind them. It makes them nervous."

"I could see that," he allowed.

"Plus, all the stiffs—er, deceased—were Cubanos. Why aren't any white people dying in this place?"

Eduardo shrugged. "I don't know what to tell you. Mr. Garcia was fine last night when Val checked on him. He was deader than a doornail at five o'clock this morning."

"Wanna take a stab at cause of death?"

"Congestive heart failure," he ventured. "It usually is."

It usually was. But the last three corpses had left the morgue with 'sudden, unexplained death' not 'congestive heart failure' or 'natural causes' written on their certificates.

The coroner was as unhappy about the uptick in business as she was, and he'd pressed her to lean harder on the nurses. As if she didn't know how to do her own blasted job. It wasn't like she told him how to do an autopsy.

But it *was* weird, any fool could see that—three, now four deaths in a month. None of the dead had been sick. Nobody fell out of bed and broke a hip, had a heart attack, caught pneumonia. They just up and died in the middle of the night with grotesque grimaces of fear pasted on their faces. But Ed didn't seem to have anything to offer her beyond they were old.

"Okay. Does Mr. Garcia have a next of kin?"

"There's a daughter in California. She's already been contacted. Said she'd leave the details to Pastor Scott's people. She trusts they'll do the right thing."

His voice was perfectly bland and neutral. But its flatness spoke volumes as to what he thought about the daughter's confidence in the church.

She sighed and stared down at poor Mister Garcia, who was already turning gray.

"Can you convince the associate pastor on call to release the body for an autopsy?"

Felicia was many things, but a diplomat was not one of them. It would be better for her, the department, and the Golden Island Church if Eduardo ran interference for her.

"I'll try. It's easier when the family wants it, though. Some of these pastors say it goes against their teachings."

"Bryce Scott doesn't seem to have a problem with it," she pointed out.

"What difference would it make to Scott? They don't hand the wallet over for an autopsy, only the corpse."

They shared a bitter, knowing laugh. Then Ed hastily made the sign of the cross, as if seeking forgiveness for his blasphemy.

"Let me call Dr. Ashland and see where he is. He ought to be here by now." Responding to calls from Golden Shores was a grade-A pain in the butt. The island was accessible only by boat or helicopter.

As she walked over to the window to get better cell phone reception, she caught a glimpse of the ornate gold crucifix nailed over Mr. Garcia's bed. Then her eyes fell on the small statue of Saint Francis of Assisi on the bedside table.

"Hey, Ed?"

"Hmm." He looked up from the notes he was typing into the iPad he'd wheeled in on his cart.

"These guys are okay with Catholicism?" She waved her hand around the room to indicate she was talking about Bryce Scott and his followers.

Eduardo scrunched up his shoulders and pulled a face. "Kinda. I mean, there's a non-denominational chaplain here to tend to the spiritual needs of all the residents who aren't members of Scott's church. And they do let Father Rafael come over once a month and say Mass. But ..."

"But?"

"It doesn't stop them from trying to convert the residents. Or the staff, for that matter."

"Huh. Still, surprised they allow it at all." She pressed the speed dial number for the medical examiner's mobile phone.

"They tolerate it," Ed clarified.

He looked as if he were going to elaborate, so she nodded at him to go ahead. But he gave his head a small shake, pressed his lips together, and returned his attention to his chart.

CHAPTER THREE

B odhi King squatted and studied the leaf he held lightly between two fingers. It was dark green and vibrant. The plant was healthy. He released the leaf and pressed a finger into the spongy earth. The soil was healthy. Alive.

He rocked back on his heels then raised his face to the sun's warmth and closed his eyes, breathing in the life energy that coursed through the garden. He didn't know how long he'd been sitting that way, meditating on the plants. But when a shadow fell across his back, he opened his eyes and turned around.

"You're a hard man to find."

Bodhi stood and brushed the dirt off his hands before clasping his visitor on the back.

"And yet you found me." He softened the words with a smile.

Allegheny County Coroner Saul David returned the smile, but Bodhi noted the strain in the man's eyes.

"Come inside. I'll make us some tea."

Saul followed him up onto the porch and then into the kitchen of the old brick farmhouse. Bodhi filled the kettle with water and put it on the stove.

Then he turned and contemplated his unexpected guest.

"How did you find me, anyway?"

"Your old next-door neighbor. I stopped by her place looking for you, and she said you were house-sitting out here. She didn't have an exact address, but there are only four farms on this road, so here I am."

"Here you are," Bodhi agreed. "Why?"

Saul smiled. "No time for tea and sympathy, huh?"

"I'll be happy to catch up all afternoon over tea. The rocking chairs on the porch are a pleasant place to catch the breeze. But I'm pretty sure the county coroner didn't drive out here in the middle of the workday to hear how the tomato plants are doing."

"Fair enough. You're right, this isn't purely a social call."

"I'm not coming back."

"I'm not here to ask you to."

Bodhi's eyes widened in mild surprise. "Really?"

"Okay, sure, I'd be thrilled if you decided to come

back. There'll always be a place for you in any forensic pathology department I'm running. But this is about something else."

The kettle whistled.

"What's it about, then, Saul? Is something wrong?"

He glided across the kitchen, taking down mugs, assembling a tray, choosing spoons. His movements were spare and fluid and didn't belie the hum of worry rising in his throat. People found him to be a calming presence in a crisis: as a result, friends seemed to seek him out to share their tragedies.

Saul had known him for a long time, though, and picked up on the frisson of concern.

"I'm fine. It's not a personal issue. I got a call from a medical examiner's office down in Florida. In the Keys."

Bodhi carried the bamboo tray of tea supplies to the table. "Here or outside?"

"Here's fine."

He sat. "And why would a call from an ME in the Florida Keys bring you to my doorstep?"

"Four sudden, unexplained deaths in a small population. They're stymied. They need someone who understands what to do about a death cluster. Apparently, when the coroner started asking around, your name came up—more than once."

Bodhi nodded. It would have. A handful of years ago, he'd traced the deaths of five young women from myocarditis to the wild red ginseng sold in a sports beverage. The case had made the national news, the medical journals, the legal journals, and a 'ripped from the headlines' episode of a popular police drama. And the spotlight had driven Bodhi from the job he'd loved.

He'd sought solitude in a series of remote locations —beginning at a banana plantation in Costa Rica and ending at a Japanese monastery in Hawaii. He was at peace, reading, house-sitting, volunteering, and meditating. The challenge of a puzzle to solve tempted him, but not enough.

"I'm not interested."

"Why not? Nobody's asking you to make a long-term commitment. It's a consulting gig. In the freaking Florida Keys. I mean, how is that not a dream job?"

"Where in the Florida Keys?—not that it matters."

"The deaths have all occurred at an assisted care facility on a private island owned by some church."

"A church owns the assisted care facility, you mean?"

"The church owns the entire island. The preacher's some television guy, Bruce or Bryce Something or Other. And the church is willing to bankroll the investigation, so we're not talking about a consulting fee that a county medical examiner has in his budget. They're willing to pay you well. Not that you care about the money," Saul hurried to add.

"You're right, I don't. But a small, insular community suffering under the strain of a spate of deaths? No, thanks. I'd be an outsider, someone to focus on."

"You're afraid they'll blame you if you can't come up with an answer?"

"I'm not worried about my reputation. I don't want the attention."

Saul rubbed his face. "Let me ask you this. Do you think you could solve it—figure out what's killing those people?"

Bodhi sat and considered the question in silence for a moment. Then he gave a small shrug. "I think I could."

He said it with no bravado. But it was the truth. He had a scientist's analytical mind for creating patterns and a priest-like ability to tease out the silent stories of the dead.

"I think so, too. So don't you have to?"

"Have to?"

Saul squinted at him through the late afternoon light that streamed through the white crocheted curtains and left lacy shadows on his face. "Yeah, what's the First Precept? The one that's basically 'thou shalt not kill'?"

"Abstain from taking life. But the precepts aren't the equivalent of the Ten Commandments."

Saul waved his hand. "Right. There are all sorts of ethical considerations, blah, blah. But the bottom line is a Buddhist shouldn't rejoice in killing, encourage killing, daydream about killing, even."

"Basically."

"And allowing these deaths to continue when you could stop them—how's that square with your precept?"

Bodhi narrowed his eyes. "You didn't say the medical examiner suspects homicide. It's an assisted care facility, after all. Dying of old age isn't tantamount to a killing."

Saul stood up, his tea untouched. "I don't have a clue if the ME knows his tuchus from a hole in the ground, to tell you the truth. But he knows something's not right, and he was smart enough to know he needs an expert. And if you ask me, no matter what's behind that death cluster down in Florida, if you can stop it and you don't, then you're taking life through your inaction."

He dropped a heavy hand on Bodhi's shoulder as

he passed the chair on his way to the door. "I'm sorry, Bodhi. It's how I feel."

He let himself out. The wooden screen door thudded silently into place. After a moment, a car engine came to life.

Bodhi stared at his hands and focused on his breath until the echo of Saul's words had faded from his ears.

CHAPTER FOUR

A rthur pressed his palms down hard against the tops of his thighs, trying to control his nerves and keep from losing his patience. He'd tried again and again to bring up his request over dinner, but his grandmother had repeatedly steered the conversation off-course.

He watched her now as she fiddled with her rosary beads. He listened to the just-audible soft music piped into the dimly lit room. He inhaled the scent of her flowery perfume.

"Arturo, I just don't understand."

He tried again to explain. "You know the church that runs this place—Pastor Scott's church?"

"Yeah, sure. The Golden Gate Church."

"No, no, *lita*, that's the bridge in California. It's the

Golden Island Church. That's the name of this island, remember?" he said as gently as he could.

"Ah, right. Golden Island, Golden Shores. Why is a man of God so worried about gold, hmm, *nieto*?"

His grandmother cocked her head to the side and watched his face, waiting for his answer.

"I suspect it's because the island is called Golden Key."

"How did you end up so naive?"

"*Lita*, this is serious. I have a business opportunity." He reached over and straightened the light cotton cardigan that had begun to slip from her shoulders.

"Atch, business, at a time like this." She mimed spitting in disgust.

"A time like what?"

She arranged her lined face into a frown. "A time of death, Arturo. Señor Garcia has died." She made the sign of the cross.

"Someone's always dying around here."

She clucked at him and murmured a prayer in rapid Spanish. At least, he thought it was a prayer. He only caught one phrase—*San Lázaro*, Saint Lazarus.

He reached for her thin hand. "I'm sorry. I shouldn't have said that."

She cast a conspiratorial glance around the otherwise-empty sunroom then whispered, "No, it's true.

There are bad spirits here. I need you to go to Miami, to a *botanica*. The good one, near the restaurant your mom used to like. Get me a seven-day *Ajo Macho* candle, a gold one if you can—to chase away evil spirits and provide protection from the evil eye. "

Now his eyes darted around the room. The last thing he needed was for her to start with her superstitious, black magic mumbo-jumbo and have someone from the church overhear her.

"Grandmother," he said loudly. "You should pray the rosary. And you don't have to wait for Father Rafael to come for Mass; watch the Golden Island service on the television. I think it will bring you a lot of comfort."

"Oh, you and your smiley-faced Pastor Scott."

He felt sweat beading on his forehead. Was she trying to get him in even more trouble with the church?

"Please, *lita*," he pleaded with her.

"Don't *lita* me. Do what I ask. Get me my garlic candle. Now, I'm tired. Please take me back to my room so I can rest until my shows come on."

Her tone was haughty, but he could hear the underlying anxiety threatening to crack through to the surface.

"What about my business opportunity? You

haven't let me explain. Pastor Scott is opening up a limited number of positions for people to join the Spread the Word Ministry. I've been chosen."

"That's nice for you, *nieto*. It's good money, like the computer job?"

"It's not about the money, It's about spreading the Good Word. But yes, the compensation is very generous. Better than the computer job. It's like ... a franchise. I would be an owner. But, I need to buy in. To make an investment. That's why I thought ..."

He trailed off as she reached for her handbag. His heart thudded. She was going to do it. She was going to write him a check. He could feel his palms growing damp with anticipation.

She rifled inside and removed her beaded change purse. She unsnapped the closure and carefully took out two folded ten-dollar bills.

"When you go to get the candle, get one for yourself, too. The red *San Sebastian*. It brings luck and prosperity to business."

She proffered the creased bills with a wide smile. He stared at her in disbelief as she pressed the money into his hand. He wondered what color candle he could light to make her stop with her ignorant nonsense and take him seriously. She had the money. She could give it to him—call it a loan, a gift, he didn't care which. He'd make it back a hundred-fold.

He opened his mouth and might have said something cutting, something that would have damaged their relationship beyond repair, but his words died in his throat. Raised voices calling for medical equipment rang through the hallway. The pounding of running feet echoed from every direction.

———

Bryce raced down the deserted hallway. He skidded to a stop when he reached the vortex of activity outside Esmeralda Morales's room.

"What's happened?" he demanded of the nearest medical professional.

A man, dressed in nursing scrubs, wheeled around. When he saw who'd addressed him, his eyes widened.

He stammered. "Oh, Pastor Scott. Did someone call you? They shouldn't have bothered you. There's nothing you can do."

Bryce waved his hand impatiently. "No, I was using the helipad on the roof. I have meetings tomorrow in Miami, and my plan was to go out and sleep on the mainland so I'm fresh in the morning. I heard the code called over the radio in the guard booth. What happened?"

The nurse lowered his eyes. "Esmerelda has been out of sorts ever since Carlos Garcia died. They were very friendly. They played pinochle and took water aerobics together. Some of the nurses think they might've had a romance, too. I'm not sure about that, but they were quite close. Esmeralda hasn't been sleeping well since he passed away." He hesitated.

Bryce nodded his understanding and motioned for the nurse to continue.

"She decided to skip dinner tonight and try to get some rest. One of the aides went in to check on her to see if she wanted some broth or toast and tea. She found her ... already gone."

"Have the authorities been called?"

"Yes," the nurse answered, then looked at him, awaiting more questions or some instruction.

Bryce made up his mind. "I'd like to see her."

"Uh, ... Detective Williams told me not to let anybody in the room until she gets here." The nurse's expression was pained, and his voice was apologetic.

Bryce's nostrils flared, but he managed to keep his temper in hand. "Nurse Martinez, this is my island. And if I want to go in that room, I'm going to go in."

"Yes, sir. Of course." The nurse yanked the door open and held it for him.

As he walked across the threshold, Bryce turned and said, "Thank you. I do understand you're following protocol, but I'm a man of God. It's my duty to hasten Ms. Morales's spirit on its journey to its eternal resting place in heaven."

The nurse's face was an unreadable mask. But he nodded then hung back in the doorway as Bryce crossed the room and looked down at the woman.

Esmeralda Morales had been one of the younger residents of Golden Shores. She was a spry and lively sixty-four. She really didn't fit in at the assisted care building and would have been offered a spot in one of the island's independent cottages had she not broken both of her wrists the previous summer during a jet skiing mishap.

Her physician thought, given the frailty of her bones and the advanced state of her osteoporosis, she'd be safer someplace like Golden Shores rather than on her own in her waterfront condo on Big Pine Key. But looking down at her now, Bryce wasn't convinced her doctor had been right.

Her mouth hung open. Her lips were curled back and and her eyes were wide and unfocused. Her mouth was open, contorted into an unnerving scream of fear.

Bryce had been told the other four residents had had similar terrified expressions when they had been found. But seeing it with his own eyes chilled him. He was reminded of a medieval painting of a woman confronted by a hellish demon. Reflexively, he dropped to his knees at her bedside and began to pray.

Bryce didn't know how long he stayed by her bedside with his head bowed. After a while, he recited the Lord's Prayer. Then he rose and clasped his hands in front of him, like a bridesmaid clutching a bouquet.

He took one final look at the body stretched out in the bed before turning and walking back into the hall. His movements felt jerky, awkward.

As he passed Nurse Martinez, he said, "Someone should at least close her eyes."

The nurse nodded. "The police don't want us to touch her until they've taken photographs. And the Medical Examiner's Office wants to see the body in the state in which it was found. But it's my understanding, the funeral home on Sugarloaf Key does a very nice job. I'm told the deceased always look as if they're at peace."

Bryce had no response to that assurance, so he simply said, "Good night."

He turned to walk toward the elevator and found the nurse jogging along beside him. "Wait. Pastor Scott, sir. Since you're already here, don't you think you should stay and talk to the detective. She'll be here in another twenty minutes. A half hour at the most."

Bryce checked his watch. "I can't. You know twenty minutes can turn into an hour on the Overseas Highway. Then, she'll need to take a ferry .... No, I have to get to Miami. This is an important meeting. But I'll have my office fill me in on the police investigation tomorrow."

He blasted Eduardo with the full power of his smile before turning away.

He'd only walked about fifteen feet, when he saw Arthur, the hapless unemployed IT guy, poking his head out from one of the spacious sunrooms set aside for residents to visit with family members. He stopped, genuinely surprised to see the man.

"Arthur, what are you doing here?"

Arthur looked guilty, as though he were embarrassed to be caught there. He inched his way out into the hallway.

"I'm visiting my grandmother. Is everything okay? There was a lot of commotion a little bit ago."

Bryce ignored the question. "I didn't realize you had a relative staying with us here."

"Yes, my *lita*, er, grandmother. She moved in not long after you opened the facility."

"What's her name? I don't recall seeing anyone with your surname on the list of congregants on site."

"Oh, she's my mother's mother, and she remarried. We don't share the same last name. Her name is Julia Martin."

Bryce noticed that, while Arthur had answered his question, he'd done it in a way that didn't confirm whether his maternal grandmother attended Golden Shores services. It would have been useful information to have, if only because he would have a better sense of Arthur's financial situation if he knew how much or whether his grandmother was tithing.

"Does she attend services here?" He asked point blank.

Arthur's face flushed.

But before he could answer, the door swung open, and a small, thin woman stepped out into the hall beside him.

"Who are you talking to, Arturo?"

Then she turned and fixed her alert eyes on Bryce. "Oh, Pastor Scott. What was that racket. Who's dying now?" Her tone was sharp and knowing.

And, although he had no trouble deflecting the very same question from her grandson, Bryce found himself answering the old woman. "I'm sorry to say Esmeralda Morales has passed away. May she rest in peace."

He dropped his eyes but noted that she made the sign of the cross. That answered the question of whether she worshipped at the Golden Island Church. She did not. She was one of Father Rafael's Roman Catholics.

"I was just telling my grandmother about the Spread the Word Ministry," Arthur interjected. "Wasn't I, *lita*?"

The old woman cut her eyes toward her grandson. "You were. You've been offered a franchise, I believe," she said dryly.

Bryce dialed his smile up to eleven. "I wouldn't think of it as a franchise, so much as a growing family. We're very fond of Arthur at the church. He's a great addition to our lay ministry program. And I know he could do well as an affiliate." He put a fatherly arm around the younger man.

Arthur blushed. His grandmother shot Bryce a look that indicated she was not impressed.

"'I'm afraid I have to go. My helicopter's waiting."

"What are you going to do about all these people dropping dead, Pastor Scott?" the old woman said, while at the same time Arthur was saying, "Let me walk out with you, Pastor Bryce."

Bryce blinked at them. "May God bless you both richly. But I really must leave now; I've got an important meeting in the morning."

He turned and strode down the hallway before either of them could respond. Over his shoulder, he heard Arthur's grandmother railing at him.

"Did you hear that? Another death. Esmerelda was as healthy as they come. Don't you roll your eyes at me, Arturo. I'm serious. I need that candle. With the oil to dress it to be sure it works."

The gleaming golden doors to the elevator opened, and Bryce stepped inside and allowed the car to sweep him up to the rooftop.

CHAPTER FIVE

Ardently do today what must be done.
Who knows? Tomorrow, death
comes.

THE BUDDHA,
BHADDEKARATTA SUTTA

Therefore, to him who knows to do good
and does not do it, to him it is sin.

JAMES 4:17

Bodhi remained behind in the meditation room when the others filed out on bare, silent feet. He closed his eyes and waited for peace to come—a peace that had eluded him during the group meditation.

His mind was clear. No thoughts flitted within it, niggling at him. He focused on the rhythm of his breath and the beat of his heart. He heard the chatter and song of the birds in the trees just outside the open windows. He felt the hint of a breeze ruffle his thin cotton shirt. He smelled the faint whiff of spices sneaking into the room from the curries cooking in the large kitchen at the end of the hall.

He was as present as he could be. And, still, no peace.

He sensed movement and opened his eyes. Daishin, the novice monk, sat lotus-style just at the edge of Bodhi's mat and watched him.

"You seem troubled." It was an observation devoid of judgment.

"I am."

"Wandering mind?"

"No." Bodhi shook his head, unsettled. He wasn't sure he could put into words what he was experiencing. "My mind is focused. I'm not thinking. But I feel ill at ease. Jumpy."

Daishin was quiet for a very long time before he said, "Perhaps, then, the trouble is you should be thinking."

"Come again?"

A smile creased Daishin's face. "Yes, we learn we must quiet our thoughts on the cushion so we can be mindful. But if we face a decision or a choice, sometimes we need to be mindful *of* our thoughts."

Bodhi considered this. "I am faced with a choice— or the consequences of one, at least."

"Then, I suggest you sit with it until your thinking clears and you can surrender to your decision."

Dashin unfolded his legs and stood. "The mind has no schedule, of course. But if you can achieve clarity in the next twenty minutes, please join us for lunch."

The monk extinguished the candles on the windowsill and left the room.

Bodhi resettled on his mat.

He had told Saul no. He did not want to investigate a death cluster, especially not one that would put him in the public eye, giving interviews and tiptoeing through political minefields. He wanted to garden, and read, and meditate.

His stomach tightened as he replayed his choice. He investigated the response.

Why did his stomach clench as if he were tense? What was stressful about choosing a quiet existence?

People are dying, and nobody knows why.

Death comes for us all. It's a part of life.

But I must cultivate and encourage life. Maybe Saul is right. Is refusing to help no different than taking a life?

His pulse fluttered in his throat.

Yes. It is.

Then you have to go to Florida and help.

He sat with that decision, examining how it felt. It felt uncomfortable, like a pair of too-tight shoes. He dismissed his attachment to emotional comfort. Following the precepts didn't promise a life free of trouble.

Indulgent. The word formed in his mind.

He was indulging his desires. How could he forsake physical comforts and excess but cocoon himself as if he were too delicate to face life? He couldn't, not if he sought enlightenment.

He opened his eyes. It was decided.

He would join the monks for a bowl of curry and then call Saul and tell him to offer his services to the medical examiner in the Keys.

Outside the room, he retrieved his sandals from the shoe rack by the door and removed his mobile phone from his right sandal. As he slipped it into his pocket, it vibrated in his hand to announce an incoming call.

———

Detective Felicia Williams tapped her apple red fingernails against the surface of her desk and listened to the phone ring.

C'mon, you crusty old coot. Pick up.

"Hello?"

She nearly dropped the phone. The voice that answered the number assigned to Dr. Bodhi King was gentle and welcoming. Very un-coot-like.

"I'm trying to reach Dr. Bodhi King," she said more tentatively than she would have liked.

She figured the odds were 70-30 that the Allegheny County Coroner's office had given her the wrong number. This polite guy did not sound like a cranky retiree. It was probably for the best, anyway. There'd be hell to pay if the chief found out she'd done an end run around him to help the medical examiner's office.

"You've got him."

Her nails stilled. "Really? I mean... um... Sorry, let

me start again. This is Detective Felicia Williams, calling from the Florida Keys."

"Yes? How can I help you?"

Her mind raced. She'd girded herself for a fight. She wasn't prepared for … warmth, of all things. She decided to take his question literally.

"You can help us by coming down here and investigating all these dead senior citizens," she told him in her bluntest voice.

"Okay."

She blinked. "What? I mean, could you repeat that?"

"I'll make arrangements to be there tomorrow. I'll need the address of the medical examiner's office. And I suppose someplace to stay—nothing fancy."

"I … really?"

There was a smile in his voice. "I was just meditating on this very question and had decided I should help if I could. Then you called—as if the Universe wanted to give me a nudge. Consider me nudged. Four deaths in four weeks is—"

"Five."

"Pardon?"

She put aside her surprise and said in a grim tone, "There's been a fifth death at Golden Shores. Esmeralda Morales was found last night, dead in her bed, a grimace of horror on her face."

The forensic pathologist was silent for a moment. Then he said, "I see. And has your medical examiner opined on the cause of death?"

"No, look, Dr. Ashland is doing everything by the book. But the local paper is calling for him to be fired. The families of the dead are outraged. And the Golden Island Church leadership issued a statement calling him incompetent. He's not. But he's hit a wall, and he needs some help. He needs *your* help."

"Okay."

"Good. I'll pick you up at the airport. Dr. Ashland or I will send you copies of the reports."

He took down her phone number and promised to call after he'd made his flight arrangements.

Then he said, "I'm hopeful the three of us can figure this out together, Detective Williams."

"Me, too," she murmured.

As she ended the call, Felicia realized she actually *felt* hopeful—for the first time in weeks she thought there might be a chance they'd figure out what the devil was going on at Golden Shores.

CHAPTER SIX
_____

Tension and fear gripped the Men's Advanced Bible Study Group. Bryce could smell it on their bodies—acrid and coppery. He could almost taste it.

"The Devil has got ahold of Golden Shores!" Roger Howard moaned, voicing what they'd all been thinking.

A babble of prayers and protests rose from the semi-circle of men gathered around the fire pit.

Bryce had to regain control of them. For the briefest moment, he wished he were his daddy. Pastor Wilbur Scott had been a fire-and-brimstone preacher. A snake handler. And a speaker of tongues. Back in the day, he'd traveled the state, driving the devil out of Floridians from Jacksonville to Key West and every-where in between.

But Bryce was not his daddy. He'd never performed an exorcism. Or hollered at a crowd of sinners to let the Holy Spirit in. Or, heaven forbid, waved around a reptile.

No. Because for all the passion Wilbur Scott had inspired among the believers at his tent revivals, he had always, always, been dirt broke. When Bryce decided to follow in his father's liturgical shoes, he'd vowed that his family wouldn't dress in rags.

The abundance gospel he preached gave his flock the keys to a life rich in blessings. It offered virtually no guidance, however, on dealing with a potential Satanic force that terrorized, tormented, and terminated senior citizens in the dead of night.

He exhaled slowly through his nose then raised his hands. "Brothers, please. It's true we're being tested. But we have to have faith. You're the elders, the most respected members of the congregation. If you panic, the others will follow. And it would be a grave detriment to the church's coffers if attendance falls off."

His soothing tone had the desired effect. In the light cast by the fire's flames, he saw several heads nodding in agreement.

He went on, "If dark forces are at work, then we need to defeat them with light and love. We've made it a point to welcome residents to Golden Shores no matter what their religious affiliation might be. And that's not going to change. But, the residents who are dying are all non-believers. That's by design—Satan's design. We have the opportunity to save souls here."

"Amen," someone shouted.

He went on, "As you know, the inaugural class of the Spread the Word Ministry is about to begin. We'll task the invitees with visiting Golden Shores, talking to the residents about God's eternal blessings, and holding some informal talks and prayer groups. We'll flood the assisted care facility with the power of God."

Ron Porter spoke first. "I like this plan, Pastor. It will give the franchisees—er, lay ministers—valuable hands-on experience before they start up their territories and may vanquish the evil that's taken up residence at Golden Shores."

Bryce smiled. As an associate director, Ron had great incentive to see the Spread the Word Ministry program succeed. After all, each of his initiates would tithe ten percent of his income directly to Ron.

"Is everyone in agreement, then?"

The men chorused 'aye' then bowed their heads. Roger led them all in a closing prayer, and they sat in prayerful silence watching the fire die down to nothing more than the glow of bright embers.

As the group broke up and started walking up the

lit path to the parking area and their cars in twos and threes, Bryce pulled Ron aside.

"Has Arthur Lopez signed his contract yet?"

Ron sighed heavily. "Not yet. He says he's going to get the buy-in funds from his grandmother."

"Julia Martin."

"You know her?"

"I met her last night. She's a resident at Golden Shores. Why don't you task Arthur with leading the outreach there?"

"Even though he hasn't met his financial obligation yet?" Ron's voice was filled with surprise and disbelief.

"Yes. I know it's not our way. And he *will* need to make his investment or he's out. But making him the face of the program at the assisted care facility might help loosen Mrs. Martin's purse strings."

Ron's laugh of appreciation rang out in the dark. "Of course. Once she sees her grandson doing ministry work, the Holy Spirit will surely move her to bless him with her money. You're a genius."

Bryce smiled modestly. "I am but the vessel, Ron. He is the genius."

CHAPTER SEVEN

The gleaming ground level of Key West International Airport was nearly empty—almost eerily deserted. Bodhi's footsteps echoed across the floor as he walked toward the baggage claim area and the lone woman who stood holding a sign that read 'Dr. King.'

She wore a severe navy blue pantsuit that matched her severe hairstyle—jet black hair pulled back and secured in a tight, neat bun at the nape of her neck. Her shoes were sensible oxfords. Her fingernails were short but painted a glossy red.

He shifted his duffle bag onto his left shoulder and stuck out his right hand. "Detective Williams?"

She let her eyes drift over him for a moment. "Yes. What can I do for you?" she asked in a clipped, impersonal tone.

"I'm Bodhi." He looked down at his still-extended hand and then at the sign.

"*You're* the retired hotshot coroner who's going to save our bacon?"

"I don't know about all that. But I *am* Bodhi King." He smiled encouragingly.

She flushed and held the sign against her left side. She gripped his outstretched hand in a firm handshake. "Sorry. I wasn't expecting a ... you don't look like ... Ah, crap—"

"It's okay. I'll bet you were expecting a distinguished, slightly portly gentleman. Balding, but with a full white beard. Right?"

"Well, yeah. Who's that?"

"That guy? As far as I know he doesn't exist. But that's who I think of when I hear 'coroner' or 'medical examiner,' too. Not a long-haired hippie-looking guy who smells like patchouli."

She threw back her head and laughed a tinkling laugh. It was an unexpectedly musical sound from someone so button-downed.

"Can we start over? Hi, Dr. King. I'm Detective Williams."

"It's a pleasure to meet you, Detective Williams. Please, call me Bodhi."

Her hesitant smile quavered. "Okay. But ..."

"I've spent lots of time with homicide police. I wouldn't dream of calling you by your first name and undermining your authority with your colleagues. I get it, Detective Williams."

Her eyes widened. "Thanks. How was your flight?"

"It was fine. The approach to the airport is gorgeous, all that brilliant blue water."

She jerked her thumb toward his canvas bag. "Did you check your luggage or is that it?"

"This is it. I travel light."

"Figures. C'mon then. Car's this way."

He fell into step beside her, and they crossed the lobby in silence. As he walked outside, the air-conditioned chill dissipated instantly and the humid Florida air dropped over him like a thick, soggy blanket.

Detective Williams removed a pair of dark sunglasses from her pocket and covered her eyes while Bodhi squinted in the bright sunlight. He was about to dig through his bag for a baseball cap to shield his eyes when he spotted a dark gray sedan with a light flashing on the roof. The sedan was parked in front of a whimsical mural of a bright yellow sun on a blue background announcing the traveler's arrival to the Conch Republic. Yellow paint along the curb and several 'loading zone, no standing' signs made clear that the car was parked illegally.

"I take it that's your car?"

Instead of answering, she reached up and removed the light then popped the trunk and passenger side door. He grabbed his Pirates hat from the duffle bag then tossed the bag into the trunk.

He slid into the seat next to Detective Williams and waited while she scrolled through her emails. She pulled out fast. As they merged into the flow of traffic, she palmed the steering wheel with one hand and cranked the air conditioning up to full blast with the other.

He considered explaining that the car wouldn't actually cool down any faster that way, but he didn't. It wasn't his place to point out another's foibles.

She accelerated, the car shot forward, and he pressed himself back against the seat.

"Okay, we've got a little better than an hour's drive up to the medical examiner's office on Crawl Key—assuming no traffic. He's going to autopsy Mr. Garcia today. Do you need to eat first?"

"No, I'm good. But don't you mean Ms. Morales? She was the most recent death, not Garcia. Right?"

During the first leg of his flight, from Pittsburgh to

Miami, he'd reviewed the file she'd emailed him. He was certain he had the order of the deaths correct.

"You're right on the order. But Esmerelda Morales's family gave permission for her autopsy right away. Doc Ashland had to go through the church to get permission to do Garcia. And they dragged their feet."

"Why? I thought they wanted to get to the bottom of these deaths. Didn't they offer to pay for an outside pathology consultant?"

She glanced over at him. "They did. But they're confused. They aren't particularly clear on their doctrine. There was some concern that the autopsy would violate their faith, ill-defined as it is."

He couldn't miss the sneer in her voice. "Isn't it a Christian church?"

"Is it? I mean, nominally yes. But it's not like any flavor of Christianity I've ever sampled. I'm Catholic," she said by way of explanation.

"I checked out their website last night—it seems like the Golden Island Church preaches a version of the prosperity gospel, right?"

Privately, he might agree with her that the principles didn't seem particularly Christ-like, but the ideas weren't unheard of in some Evangelical circles.

She shot him another look that he couldn't read.

Her eyes were obscured by the dark lenses of her sunglasses.

"I shouldn't have brought it up. One, I don't know your religious beliefs. And two, they're paying your fees. Forget I said anything." Her tone was conciliatory.

"One, I'm a Buddhist. And two, no, they're not. I declined that offer."

"I don't follow."

"If the medical examiner's office or your department can pay me a stipend, great. Otherwise, consider my services a voluntary offering."

"You're telling me you'd do this for free?"

"Yes."

They drove in silence for several miles while she chewed on this thought.

"Huh. I'm sure the bean counters can swing some kind of payment. But I'll tell you right now, your accommodations are definitely going to be downgraded from what Golden Island Church would have offered."

"I don't need anything fancy. And, my independence is pretty crucial if I'm going to help you and Dr. Ashland figure out who or what's killing all these people. So, why don't you speak freely and fill me in on the church, the island, and anything else you think I need to know?"

She didn't respond right away. After another long silence, she gestured out the window.

"We're getting close to Big Pine Key. Golden Island's just off the coast. There's ferry service to the island from the marina there. And keep an eye out for our Key Deer—they're miniature deer. They're like local celebrities."

She still hadn't answered his question, but he momentarily forgot her evasion when she slowed the car to a crawl and pointed out the window. He turned his head in time to see a white-spotted, white-tailed deer, no bigger than the average toddler, amble across the highway.

Detective Williams pushed her sunglasses up to the top of her head and grinned in the direction of the retreating doe.

"Amazing," he breathed.

"Right? There are fewer than a thousand of them left, and we sure do love them. If you have time and the inclination, you ought to check out the wildlife refuge. They'll walk right up to you in there."

Once the deer had crossed, Detective Williams gunned her engine and returned to her cruising speed.

"So, about the church?" he prompted.

The highway gave way to the breathtaking Seven Mile Bridge that stretched over the Atlantic Ocean.

With a quick motion, she reached past him and pointed through the passenger side window to a narrow bridge running parallel to the one they were speeding across.

"That's the original railroad bridge. The first Overseas Highway was retrofitted over that bridge after the railroad went bankrupt and sold the railway to the state. Old timers say it was so narrow it was really only a lane and a half wide, so if there was a truck coming in the opposite direction, you'd have to put it in reverse and back up to the prior island and then start over."

"Is that true?"

She shrugged. "It's what they say. And there were no guardrails on that thing."

He turned his head. "There are now."

"Sure. Because now tourists ride their bikes along it and fish off it. It wouldn't do for some mainlander to take a tumble. That'd be bad for business."

She wasn't making idle chitchat. She was clearly gearing up to tell him something. He watched the late afternoon sun shimmer silver on the water for a moment.

"Are you a native of the Keys?"

"Sure am. Proud Conch." From behind the

sunglasses, her eyes flickered to his. "We're independent folks. Some natives can be insular, a little tribal, maybe. Not everyone appreciates outsiders—even if our economy does rely on tourism."

He nodded his understanding but didn't speak. He wanted her to keep talking until she got to her point.

"So maybe that's why some people have their doubts about Pastor Scott and Golden Shores. He's a transplant by way of Tallahassee. Not everybody trusts him—or the Golden Island Church. Now, granted lots of folks do. He's got something like ten thousand members in that church."

"All living in the Keys?"

She laughed. "No, not by a long shot. Loads of people travel down from the mainland for his services. Or watch the cable broadcasts. I hear that after the church bought the island, Pastor Scott came up with a plan to open a bunch of satellite centers across the state and eventually throughout the entire Southeast."

"That's ambitious."

"Right. And that kind of naked ambition doesn't sit well with everyone. Me included, to be honest. If you ask me, a church has no business buying a private island."

"So bad publicity for Golden Shores—say the kind

that comes with a flurry of dead residents—might make some people happy?"

"It might. And some of those people rubbing their hands in glee work in local government. Not Doctor Ashland. He's baffled and seems genuinely bothered by the deaths. But my boss—the chief of police—and the county commissioners, they're tickled pink that Scott's reputation is tarnished." She dropped her voice to a fierce near-whisper. "I'm pretty sure I've been assigned to all cases that arise on Golden Island because they don't think I can solve them. Which suits them fine."

Bodhi gazed out at the horizon while he considered this theory. He could believe she was being set up to fail—a woman in a man's world wasn't always welcome even in the twenty-first century. But she seemed to be hinting at something more. More political, more scandalous.

"Do you think a county official is responsible for the deaths, detective?"

She stiffened her shoulders, surprised by his directness. "Maybe. It seems farfetched. But someone's killing those people."

"Or something."

"What kind of something? Please tell me *you* aren't going to start babbling about the Devil, too."

"The Devil, as in Satan?" he asked in confusion.

"Yeah. I grew up with one of the Golden Shores nurses. He says Pastor Scott is sending in a team of assistant ministers to provide spiritual counseling to the residents. The topic of the first session, according to my nurse friend, is supposed to be how to protect oneself from the Devil."

"Don't keep me in suspense, detective. How do we protect ourselves from the Devil?"

She laughed her melodic laugh. "By making an offering, of course. In return, God will bless you with His protection."

"A cash offering, you mean?"

"I'm sure Golden Island will also take a check or credit card. But yes, they're going to be recommending that these frightened folks ward off the boogeyman by making a financial gift to the church."

The theology wasn't particularly sophisticated, but it also wasn't far off from standard religious practices. After all, part of the point of believing, in having faith, was the expectation that the higher power you prayed to would protect you.

Detective Williams interrupted his musing. "Do Buddhists believe in Satan?"

"Strictly speaking, no."

"What about loosely speaking?"

He eyed her. "How much do you want to know? It's complicated, and I can be a bit of a pedant."

She grinned. "What kind of pathologist would you be if you weren't? Coroners and lawyers—never saw anybody else so in love with hemming and hawing, qualifying and overexplaining."

He ducked his head. "That's fair. But, seriously, do you want to the short version or the long version?"

She checked the time. "Give me the medium version. We're about twenty minutes from the ME's office."

"Okay. So, traditional Buddhism acknowledges Mara, a devil or demon who confronted the Buddha. Most scholars would tell you Mara isn't purely evil or bad as the demons are portrayed in monotheistic religions. There simply aren't those sorts of absolutes in Buddhism."

"Hmm. No absolutes at all?"

"Everything is interrelated and impermanent, so no. In Buddhism, the outcome of someone's encounter with a so-called demon would depend on how enlightened that person was. But, as Buddhism spread, Asian spirits ended up being syncretized into the belief system."

"What kind of spirits—evil spirits?"

"Well, not really. More like powerful, ancient

spirits of the natural world. They had to be recognized and appeased."

"How?"

"It depends, but mainly through meditation and offerings of food, money, maybe some candles."

"Sounds like Santería," she said more to herself than to him.

"Pardon?"

"Oh, I said it sounds like the saints. The women in my family were always praying to the saints for this or that. You know, with the candles."

Her radio crackled to life: "Williams, this is Dispatch. Doc wants to know an ETA."

Detective Williams made a male masturbatory gesture with her right hand. "Ten, maybe fifteen, minutes. Why? Does the stiff have somewhere to be?"

The dispatch operator cackled. "No, but you know happy hour's about to start at Mangrove Mama's down on Sugarloaf Key. His favorite jam band plays on Tuesdays."

"Does Doctor Ashland have a large staff?" asked Bodhi.

"Ha. No. He has a part-time secretary. He's an independent contractor, not a county employee. So any staff salaries would come out of his pocket. He hires body teams to pick up the corpses—the lowest bid wins."

"No pathology fellows or medical students, then?"

"Nope. Just Doc."

Bodhi wondered how this would go. His experience at the Allegheny County Coroner's Office was unusual, he knew. Only populous cities could afford to have full-time, professional medical examiners and coroners. And fewer still could swing state-of-the-art, on-site forensics laboratories.

He could only hope Doctor Ashland's ego wasn't too fragile. The God Complex so common among physicians was downright endemic among medical examiners. He'd always figured it was because they dealt exclusively in death.

CHAPTER EIGHT

Arthur kept his head down and rushed into the *botanica*. The competing scents of burning candles, fragrant oils, and pungent herbs filled his nostrils instantly. The cramped interior was warm and stuffy, intensifying the flow of sweat down his back.

At the tinkle of the bell, the woman behind the counter looked up from her cell phone and greeted him in a bored tone. He muttered a hello without raising his head. He rushed to the shelves filled with seven-day candles of every conceivable color, which promised to solve every imaginable problem or to bestow luck, money, love, strength, children, beauty, or any combination thereof.

He grabbed the *Ajo Macho* candle his grand-mother had requested and turned to speed-walk to the cash register. As he strode off, his sleeve brushed a candle and knocked it off the shelf.

He reflexively caught the falling candle with his free hand. As he reached out to return it to the shelf, he saw the name imprinted on the label. He was holding the red *San Sebastian* candle his grandmother had said would bring him luck and prosperity in business ventures.

He stared at it for a several seconds. Then he continued on his way to the counter, now with a candle in each hand. It wouldn't do to ignore a sign from Saint Sebastian. Arthur may not have been superstitious, but he also wasn't stupid.

"Find everything okay?" the cashier asked.

"Yes." He wished she'd hurry before anyone he knew saw him in here.

She keyed in the price for each candle. Then she wrapped each of the glass candle holders in stiff brown paper before arranging them carefully in a thin plastic bag.

"You sure you don't want to get the oils, too?" she asked in a voice that left no doubt how she felt about such a foolish oversight.

His grandmother had wanted the extras, but the upsell rubbed him the wrong way.

"Why would I need them? Aren't the candles supposed to work on their own?"

She arched a brow. "Of course, they'll work. But if you prepare them and anoint them, you'll intensify their power. I guess it just depends on how much business success you want—or how strong the bad spirit is."

"What bad spirit?"

"Whatever spirit it is that has you worried. That's what this gold male garlic candle's for—protection from evil forces. You know, demons, enemies, negativity, all that stuff. Of course, if you want to protect yourself from something really malevolent, you'll need to make a real offering."

"Uh, sure. Let's add the oils."

She pawed through a drawer behind the counter and dug out the additional items. He watched her drop them into the bag and ring them up on the register.

"When you say to make an offering, you're talking about setting out coins, right?"

She twisted her full mouth into a bow of disbelief. "Brother, if you have a serious problem, you're gonna need a serious solution. I'm not talking about some coins. I'm talking about a sacrifice. A chicken. Maybe two. You know a guy? Because if not, I can give you a name of a—"

"Forget it." He pushed his grandmother's two

crumpled tens and a crisp ten-dollar bill of his own into the woman's hand and grabbed the bag.

He was halfway out the door when she called out after him that he forgot his change.

He ignored her and raced outside.

Pastor Bryce had decreed that Golden Shores was in the grip of Satanic forces. That was a serious problem, which was why Arthur had reluctantly come to the *botanica* in the first place.

He knew once he talked to the residents about the devil's presence, they'd panic. And his grandmother would be one of the worst. She could burn a candle, and he'd convince her to make a generous donation to the Golden Island Church.

But there were limits. And decapitating a chicken and spilling its blood were off limits.

He bowed his head and prayed.

CHAPTER NINE

For the living know that they will die;
But the dead know nothing,
And they have no more reward,
For the memory of them is forgotten.

ECCLESIASTES 9:5

The world is afflicted by death and
decay. But the wise do not grieve,
having realized the nature of
the world.

THE BUDDHA, SUTTA NIPATA

Doctor Joel Ashland was a sturdily built, silver-haired man with a deep tan and bright blue eyes. He wasn't quite out of coroner central casting, though, because he wore his hair in a long, low ponytail, and his white laboratory coat covered a faded Hawaiian shirt. A pair of floral board shorts in a clashing pattern and a pair of blue plastic Croc shoes completed his ensemble. Diamond studs sparkled in his earlobes.

"I'm so glad you're here," he enthused before Detective Williams had made the introductions.

After a brisk handshake and an exchange of pleasantries with Dr. Ashland, Bodhi turned to her and whispered, "*This* guy is your county's medical examiner and you expected me to be staid and conservative?"

She smiled. "I always imagined Doc here was one of a kind. I guess you're more like a matched set of hippies—although your fashion sense is better."

He laughed.

Dr. Ashland had turned away to gather some files from his cluttered desk. He looked over his shoulder. "What'd I miss?"

"Oh, just Detective Williams telling me a joke."

"Impossible. Felicia doesn't kid around. She's all business, all the time."

Detective Williams made a sour face, and the medical examiner winked at her.

He picked up a glass candy dish from his desk. "Anybody want a ginger candy before we go in?"

"No, thanks," Detective Williams said.

Bodhi shook his head and watched Dr. Ashland unwrap a piece of candy and pop it into his mouth.

"Ginger? You get nauseous?"

Dr. Ashland smiled. "Crazy, huh? You'd think after all these years, I'd be unfazed. And maybe I would. I truly don't know. But after I puked in the observation theater as a med student, a resident gave me the ginger tip. And I've been sure to have some every time. It's probably more of a superstition than anything at this point."

Bodhi considered how a man who'd vomited at the sight of an autopsy would choose a path that focused on corpses to the exclusion of everything else.

"Wait—those candies will keep my stomach from getting upset?" Detective Williams demanded.

"Ginger is known to settle the stomach," Bodhi explained.

She reached over and plucked a candy from the

dish. "Doc here never mentioned that. I thought he was just a candy-loving weirdo."

"That, too," Dr. Ashland said with a laugh. He tucked his file under his arm and gestured toward the door. "Well, shall we?"

As they walked into the hallway, he turned to Bodhi. "Do you want to lend a hand?"

So much for the egotistical medical examiner.

B odhi glanced at Detective Williams, who had stationed herself against the wall in the corner of the room closest to the door. It was a well-chosen spot: she'd be out of the way, and she had a solid surface to lean against if she started to feel faint. She was covered head-to-toe in a paper cap, paper mask, surgical gown, and booties over her shoes. Her pupils were dilated, but her skin color—what little he could see between her forehead and cheekbones —was good.

He turned his attention back to the body on the metal tray. It had been four years since he'd performed his last autopsy. When he looked down at the corpse, he saw twenty-two-year-old Jasmine Courtland, the third of five young women to die after drinking a popular energy drink. He pictured her long, flame-red curly hair and her porcelain, freckle-dotted skin.

He blinked his eyes behind the protective visor, and Jasmine Courtland dematerialized. Carlos Garcia, age eighty and still dressed in his striped pajamas, came into focus.

Dr. Ashland turned on his digital camera and photographed Carlos Garcia, taking care to get a close up of the identifying toe tag dangling from the left big toe. He moved up the body slowly from the feet to the head, taking a series of close up shots.

Then he nodded to Bodhi, who slid his double-gloved hands under the old man's thin shoulder and hip and turned the corpse onto its stomach. Dr. Ashland took another dozen photographs of the back, working his way from head to feet. When the medical examiner finished documenting the corpse's condition, Bodhi returned it to a face up position.

He helped the medical examiner ease off the blue-and-white pajamas. Dr. Ashland bagged the clothing in a pre-labeled evidence bag and sealed it then resumed his picture taking. Bodhi eased the naked body from front to back and then back to front.

"No visible signs of trauma," Dr. Ashland remarked.

"Unless you count that grimace," Bodhi countered.

They stared down in mutual silence at the rictus of horror, etched forever on Carlos Garcia's face. It was a grotesque death mask. His lips were pulled back to reveal pale gums and a partial set of teeth. His brow was furrowed and his sightless eyes were wide.

"Get a good closeup of that, would you, Doc?" Detective Williams said in a muffled voice from behind her mask.

Dr. Ashland nodded and aimed his camera at Carlos Garcia's face.

"It's the same expression as the others. Have you ever seen anything like it?"

Bodhi shook his head. "No, never. I did once see a corpse that had been infected with *Clostridium tetani*. Tetanus," he added for Detective Williams's benefit. "It had a somewhat similar expression. But it was more of an exaggerated grin. And, of course, the entire body was contorted and rigid."

"The rictus grin," Dr. Ashland said with a nod of agreement. "None of the deceased showed any signs of tetanus."

Bodhi half-listened while Dr. Ashland recorded Carlos Garcia's weight and length.

"Do you have your toxicology results back on any of the deceased?" he asked.

"Not yet."

Detective Williams growled in frustration.

Dr. Ashland turned to her. "I know. I asked the lab to put a rush on them. It might be another day or two, though. I'm also waiting on radiology reports. I don't have a mass spectrometer. What are you thinking —poisoning?"

"Right. I've never seen it. But I've read about a case of strychnine poisoning. It produces the rictus grin, too."

"Strychnine ..." Dr. Ashland mused.

"How would that be administered?" Detective Williams asked.

"It could be mixed into a drink or medication. Or administered intravenously," Bodhi said.

Dr. Ashland shook his head. "None of the dead had IV lines."

"So it would have been ingested orally?" Detective Williams asked.

"Or injected," Dr. Ashland mused.

"Or inhaled. But presumably powder would have had a more widespread effect," Bodhi offered.

"How would somebody get his or her hands on strychnine? Is it easy to come by?"

"Sure," Dr. Ashland said. "It's rat poison."

"What are you thinking? A nurse or aide with Munchausen by proxy?" Bodhi asked.

"That's the syndrome where a caregiver deliberately makes one of his or her charges sick, right? Usually the perpetrator's a woman," Detective Williams offered.

"It's certainly a possibility. Felicia, have you looked at the schedules at Golden Island to see if any of the personnel were working during the times of all five deaths?" Dr. Ashland asked.

Detective Williams rolled her eyes. "Gee, why didn't I think of that, Doc?"

Bodhi was still pondering the poisoning theory. "I'd expect the bodies to be unnaturally rigid in the case of strychnine poisoning." He glanced at the medical examiner.

Dr. Ashland shrugged. "All of them except the last one died overnight, so they were already stiff when they were found."

"And Ms. Morales?"

"Not really," Detective Williams answered. "She was kind of limp, actually. And she was still warm when I got there."

After a brief silence, Dr. Ashland said in a cheery voice, "Well, we'll know soon enough—once the toxicology tests come back. On that note, let's get some juice out of these eyeballs."

He held up a syringe attached to a 20-gauge needle and aimed it into the globe of the corpse's right eye. While the medical examiner gradually eased out the clear vitreous fluid, Bodhi glanced at Williams. Her eyes were closed and she had her head pressed back against the wall.

The vitreous fluid always seemed to get to people. That and taking the blood sample from the heart. Bodhi guessed that the invasions of the eyeball and the heart seemed somehow more real, more visceral, to observers than did the more mechanical operations of making the Y-incision, sawing apart the ribcage, and removing the individual organs.

Dr. Ashland worked efficiently and neatly. Bodhi found himself meditating on the meager drops of blood that splashed onto the tray as Dr. Ashland made two deep diagonal cuts from the corpse's shoulders to his sternum. With a steady hand, he made the third cut at the intersection of the first two—forming the tail of the "Y" that traveled down the chest to the abdomen.

Bodhi scanned the white cloth that held the medical examiner's instruments. "I don't see a rib saw," he remarked.

Dr. Ashland shook his head. "I prefer rib cutters—

well, shears, to be precise. Could you pass them to me?"

Bodhi selected a pair of shears that he was fairly certain were ordinary gardening shears and pressed them into the medical examiner's open palm. While Dr. Ashland snipped away at the ribs, he provided a running commentary of Mr. Garcia's medical condition when he was living.

"He had some moderate arthritis in his knees. High blood pressure. A mole on his neck that his doctor was keeping an eye on. But, overall, he was in pretty good health for an octogenarian."

Bodhi helped him remove the pieces of the rib cage so he could examine the organs *in situ* before removing them one by one.

After he inspected each organ, he passed it to Bodhi to have a look before depositing it into a deep stainless steel bowl.

Bodhi hefted Mr. Garcia's wet heart and turned it in his hand.

"No visible evidence of edema or hemorrhage," Bodhi noted. "Will you be preparing tissue slides for a histological analysis?"

"Sure. But realistically, by the time I get the results from histology, there could be another three or four deaths. I'll have bodies stacked up like cordwood. I'll tell you right now what we're going to find. Mr. Garcia's body will show the wear and tear associated with eight decades on this planet. But I won't be able to point to suffocation or internal bleeding or anything as the cause of death."

Bodhi noted the frustration in the medical examiner's voice. "I hear you. I can tell that you're perplexed. Maybe they really are just dying of natural causes. You are talking about a geriatric population, after all."

Dr. Ashland shook his head. "Not with those expressions. Look, something's going on there. I know it. It's something non-obvious. That's why we need you."

From the corner of the room, Detective Williams interjected. "He's right. It's too weird. It's not like Golden Shores is the only retirement community in the Keys. None of the others are averaging one unexplained death a week. And all these deceased, they're all Cuban-Americans. No white people are dying there. No black people. Nobody but Cubans. And before you ask, I don't think Cuban-Americans make up the majority population at Golden Shores. Most of the residents are Caucasians and members of the Golden Island Church."

"Okay. It's possible that there's some environmental cause of death that could be fatal for people who share a certain ethnic background—some agent that's interacting with a genetic mutation in Cuban-Americans, for example."

"How would you find out?" Dr. Ashland asked.

Bodhi exhaled, his breath hot inside his surgical mask. "If you really don't want to wait for your lab results to come in, I'd recommend doing a field study. I could go to Golden Shores and—"

"Go now, please. They'll cooperate with you. The church leadership seems to think I just fell off the turnip truck, so to speak." There was an unmistakeable note of desperation in his voice.

Bodhi looked at Detective Williams. "I'll go just as soon as Detective Williams can take me. She's my ride."

"Let's do it. I'll call ahead from the car. They'll probably have their private boat waiting for us." She pulled her mask down and let it hang around her neck.

As she reached for the door, he said, "Wait. Don't you have to stay and witness the autopsy?"

She exchanged looks with Dr. Ashland. He cleared his throat and said, "I'm recording it on the iPad. I think the pressing public health concerns outweigh the need to follow procedure exactly here, don't you, Detective Williams?"

"Agreed. And I know the chief would feel the same."

Bodhi shrugged. He wasn't here to police the police. "Lead the way."

"Stop by Mangrove Mama's later. I'll get a table, and we can chat," Dr. Ashland said, waving Mr. Garcia's liver for emphasis before depositing it into the bowl with a splash.

CHAPTER TEN

B ryce ended the phone call and pocketed his cell phone. He turned to Cleo Clarkson, the director of Golden Shores and his right-hand woman.

"That was the chief of police. He's sending that lady detective over with the forensic pathologist. Have the boat captain meet them at the Big Pine dock after he drops me at the compound."

The faintest furrow materialized on her smooth brow. "The forensic pathologist? Does he mean the medical examiner, Dr. Ashland?"

"No. It's the fellow from Pittsburgh."

She shook her head in confusion, and her glossy brown hair bounced against her shoulders, releasing an invisible cloud of floral-scented shampoo.

She was exquisite. Stunning didn't do her justice.

Bryce's enter career was built on the appeal of luxury and wealth. He was expected to surround himself with beautiful things and beautiful women. And she was one of God's perfect creations, the gorgeous face of Golden Shores.

Bryce deeply loved his wife of seventeen years and would never be unfaithful to her. She was his rock, a woman of great faith and steadiness. But he was a man of flesh and couldn't deny the effect Cleo's beauty had on him. The fact that she was in her early thirties only compounded his secret guilt.

"Bryce, I was sure I told you Dr. King declined our invitation to consult on the deaths." Her throaty voice took on a note of apology.

"You did. But he apparently agreed to Dr. Ashland's request for help. He wanted to maintain his independence."

She frowned. "I wouldn't dream of trying to influence him."

"I know." He gave her shoulder a quick squeeze of reassurance, noting how the fine silk of her blouse felt like liquid under his fingers. "But it's probably better this way. A blessing. Now no one will question his findings."

"Hmm, I suppose."

"I'm certain of it. Please be sure to accommodate him however you can."

"Of course." She smiled languidly.

He checked the time on his heavy gold watch and frowned. "I need to run. Oh—have you heard back from Father Rafael?"

"I have." Her eyes dropped to her desk and she paused, as if searching for a way to break the news. "He says there are very specific rules about when a Roman Catholic priest can perform an exorcism, which would require an investigation by the local bishop. But the biggest hurdle, he says, is that the rite of exorcism has to be performed on a *person*. A practicing Roman Catholic who's suffering from demonic possession. He can't exorcise the building."

Bryce sighed. He'd had high hopes that the priest could help calm the residents' fears. Because his lay ministers had only succeeded in whipping up their panic—and loosening their purse strings. Arthur's most recent meeting had resulted in more than two thousand dollars in donations, but the center was on the verge of mass hysteria.

Cleo made a small noise in her throat. "He did suggest we contact a local *santero*. He can give me a name if you're open to that."

He didn't recognize the word. "I'm sorry, *santero* means what?"

Another throat-clearing noise from Cleo. Then, "A Santería priest. My understanding is that a *santero* could perform a protective ritual and—"

"Absolutely not. Catholicism is one thing, Cleo. I will not endorse paganism." He bristled at the thought.

"Of course not," she heard the undercurrent of anger in his voice and hurried to placate him. "But Santería's quite closely tied to the Roman Catholic faith among Afro-Cubans and Cubanos. And it might help to—"

"No."

She pressed her lips into a firm, thin line. "Understood."

"Good. Now, I have to go. Please keep me in the loop on Dr. King's investigation."

"I will," she promised.

He allowed himself one last look at her. The wide collar of her blouse revealed the delicate skin at the base of her throat and gave just a glimpse of her upper chest. She was flushed, probably in response to being rebuked. But the color gave the illusion that she was aroused.

He swallowed hard and hurried out of her office before his sinful imagination could take hold. He considered that perhaps *he* was a candidate for exorcism.

———

Cleo pasted her brightest smile on her face and circulated through the halls. She made it a point to visit with each of her one hundred and forty residents, whom she considered and called her 'guests,' at least a few times each week.

Her first stop was Mr. Santiago's room. When she popped her head in, he looked up and grinned.

She waited, as she always did, for him to close the book he was reading and motion for her to come inside and sit. Cleo insisted she didn't have favorites among the residents. But, for many reasons, she was especially fond of Hector Santiago.

"How are you doing today?" she asked as she situated herself in the deep chair across from his.

The two matching chairs filled the space near his largest window; he referred to the reading nook as his library. But he'd shown her pictures of the actual library he'd once maintained in his home—it was vast, and crammed from ceiling to floor with books.

This wasn't quite the same. But then, she knew nothing about moving into a facility was quite the same, no matter how much she tried to make the center seem homelike and comfortable.

In answer to her question, he shrugged. "I'm still kicking. Which, given recent events, seems to be something to crow about."

Her heart squeezed. "I know it must be very stressful, seeing so many of your friends pass on."

"Eh." He shrugged philosophically. "At my age, Cleo, I expect my friends to, as you say, pass with some regularity."

She nodded. It might have sounded crass to an outsider, but her guests were fairly sanguine about death.

A shadow passed over his face, and he shook his head. "I'll be honest with you. What's worrying is the stories I hear that folks are going into the great beyond, not with the blissful expression of someone who's just drifted off to sleep and never woke up, but with screams of horror etched across their faces."

He was watching closely for her reaction. She let out a long, slow breath to still her nerves before answering.

"I wouldn't put too much stock in idle chitchat by people who would have no way of knowing," she said gently.

"Neither would I. But I think the night nurses know what they're talking about."

Anger flared hot in Cleo's belly.

"Are you saying the nurses have been talking to you about this tragic situation?" she asked in a deliberately neutral tone.

Surely her nursing professionals knew better than to speak out of turn about residents' deaths to their fellow guests.

He slapped his thigh and roared with laughter. "Oh, Cleo. No, of course not. But they do love to gossip amongst themselves. Me, I'm just a wrinkled old man. I'm no more interesting to them than that potted fern on the table. You can't even imagine the things they talk about in front of me. Would you like to know all about Nurse Gallinski's symptoms of perimenopause?"

"Good Lord, no." She gave a theatrical shudder, and he chuckled.

When he'd finished laughing, she reached over and closed her hand over his. "I promise you, I'm doing everything I can to figure out what's happening."

"I'm sure you are. Just hurry up about it, would you?" He squeezed her hand tightly.

"I'll try. I should let you get back to your book and

enjoy the peace and quiet before dinner. I know this is your favorite time to read."

"I always enjoy our talks, but I admit I am at a good point in this one."

He tapped the cover, and she glanced down to see what Mr. Santiago was reading now. He had varied tastes in books. Today's selection was a thick biography of a World War II general.

"I'll leave you to it." She stood and headed toward the door.

"Stop by tomorrow and I'll let you know how it turns out. I'm planning to stay up all night and read. Seems to be the safest way to pass the overnight hours."

She was glad her back was to him, so he couldn't see her wince at his words.

Even while she listened to Mrs. Martin report proudly on her grandson Arthur's new business venture and Magdalena Carson share a caramel brownie recipe that she just had to try, part of her mind was on Mr. Santiago's words.

None of her guests seemed to notice her distraction until she reached Lynette Johnson's room.

Lynette had been one of the first black, female attorneys in the state. She was chock full of colorful war stories about murderous clients and lecherous drunk judges, and usually Cleo left her room with her stomach muscles aching from laughing so hard.

Lynette interrupted her own story about her first Supreme Court argument and demanded shrewdly, "What's wrong?"

Cleo blinked. "Nothing."

"Look here, girlie. Don't con a con man; don't BS a BSer, and don't lie to a lawyer."

"Shouldn't that be don't lie to a liar?"

Lynette raised one eyebrow comically high. "Same difference. But don't go changing the subject. Tell me what's bothering you."

"What makes you so sure something's bothering me?" Cleo asked lightly.

Lynette held up one hand and ticked off points on her be-ringed fingers. "One, you've asked me about my yoga class twice now. Two, you keep playing with the earring in your right ear, rubbing it between your forefinger and thumb. Do you know what that's called?"

Cleo hastily dropped her hand, which had in fact been headed toward her earlobe. "No."

"It's called worrying. You're worrying your earring. Pretty apt name, don't you think? Also it's a tell. You should never play cards for money."

Cleo gave a weak laugh.

Lynette went on with her list. "Three, that money-grubbing televangelist was in your office today. I saw him when I was coming back from the cooking class. He never brings good news, does he?"

"Mrs. Johnson, you know that Pastor Scott is deeply concerned about—"

"Save the defense of your boss for someone who'll buy it, missy. Your Pastor Scott is deeply concerned about the size of his bank account and not much else. And four, you're running a joint where people are turning up dead on a frequent basis. Folks are panicking, wondering if they're going to die next. Rumors of everything from a nurse with an angel of death complex to evil spirits to mob hits are flying around this place."

Cleo cocked her head. "Mob hits? I haven't heard that one yet."

Lynette waved a hand. "Oh, that's Pete Green's pet theory. Of course, Pete's also the guy who sends around chain emails promising that Steve Jobs will give everyone in America a free iPad. And it doesn't matter how many times I've reminded him that Steve Jobs is six feet under. He's still waiting for that iPad to show up from a zombie. So, consider the source on the assassination theory."

Cleo smiled wryly. "It's true enough that things are a little tense among the administrators. We certainly don't like to see guests dying. And we're sort of at a loss to figure out why."

She was surprised to hear such an honest admission of her concerns tumble from her mouth, but Lynette Johnson seem to have that effect on people.

Lynette nodded sagely. "I know. And it scares the bejeezus out of me."

Cleo was equally stunned to hear Lynette admit her fear. "We're doing everything we can," she promised lamely.

After a moment, Lynette said, "Well, I expect that fancy forensics consultant who came in from the Northeast might be able to help shed some light as to what's going on around here."

"How did you ...?" she trailed off as Lynette cackled.

"I never burn my sources, honey. But looks like the boat's coming into the dock now. You might want to hustle down there and meet them."

She nodded toward her window, which overlooked the water, and Cleo followed her gaze. Sure enough *The Golden Seas,* Golden Shores' yacht, was docking.

Leave it to Lynette to be as plugged in at Golden Shores as she'd surely been with the county criminal court back in her heyday.

"You have a nice afternoon, Lynette. And don't

worry, I promise, we're going to get to the bottom of this." She locked eyes with the older woman.

Lynette regarded her for several long seconds, her dark brown eyes intense.

"I expect you will. In the meantime, I'm sticking with my bottled water and meals I have ordered in from the mainland, thank you very much. And I'll just keep good old Saint Lazarus here handy." She patted her statue of the saint.

Cleo smiled then hurried down the hallway to the elevator so that she could meet Dr. King and that snappish police detective when they disembarked.

CHAPTER ELEVEN

Bodhi and Detective Williams passed the short ride from Big Pine Key to Golden Island above deck. She pointed out the ubiquitous mangrove stands lining the coasts of the islands they sped past and explained the tree's affinity for saltwater. Some of the details were lost as the wind and the spray carried her voice away, but he heard enough to get the gist. From what he gathered, there were four species of mangroves in the Keys, with the red mangroves growing closest to the water.

The combination of native pride and relaxed authority that crept into Detective Williams's voice when she talked about the Florida Keys made her seem softer, almost friendly. But when the captain had docked the boat and an official-looking woman in flowing linen slacks and a jewel-colored silk blouse came clattering down the dock on cream-colored high heels, Detective Williams shifted back into her prickly and brusque persona as if she were putting on a sweater.

The woman on the dock smiled widely and extended her hand before Bodhi had taken his first step off the boat.

"Dr. King, we're so glad you decided to come. I'm Cleo Clarkson. I'm the director of resident life here, which makes me the senior administrator in charge of Golden Shores."

She completely disregarded Detective Williams.

The slight apparently hadn't escaped Detective Williams's notice either. "You're doing a heckuva job at it."

Cleo Clarkson turned and said in an offhand voice, "Oh, I didn't notice you there, detective."

Detective Williams was stone-faced, but her entire body seemed to shimmer with resentment.

As the three of them made their way from the dock to a wide, paved path lined with seashells and riotously blooming tropical flowers on both sides, the director pointed out amenities ranging from the nine-hole executive golf course to the pickleball court to a lap pool.

"As you can see we offer a full complement of activities."

"Do they get much use?" Bodhi asked.

"Of course. Golden Shores offers a complete array of senior living options—from cottages for our independent living community members to assisted living apartments to suites in the skilled nursing care facility, or as people insist on calling it, the nursing home."

"I see. I wasn't aware there were so many levels of care here."

"Likely because the deaths have all occurred in the assisted care facility. The guests who stay there may need help with some tasks or require daily medications. Or they may just prefer the social aspects of the facility to living alone. We provide light nursing care and cleaning services along with a full-service restaurant and shuttle service throughout the Keys. But there's not the level of medical care there that we have in the skilled nursing care building," she explained.

So the death cluster was centered in a community within a community.

He gazed around at the sparkling blue water that surrounded the campus. "It's just so hard to imagine an entire island for a retirement community."

She seemed to stiffen almost imperceptibly. But he must have imagined it, because when she spoke her voice had the same cheerful, professional tour guide timbre.

"I suppose it's not typical. But then nothing about Golden Island is typical. The island isn't just home to the Golden Shores campus. There's the church, of course. And there are other buildings that support the church in its mission, including an event center for the use of the congregation, which we also allow outside groups to rent."

"By 'event center', she means stadium," Detective Williams interjected. "Or would you call it an arena, Ms. Clarkson?"

"It's quite a large venue," she allowed.

"It must be very expensive to live here."

"Actually, no. Because the church is a non-profit entity and Golden Shores is an arm of its ministry, we're able to keep the fees down. It's elegant and beautiful, but it's within the reach of most of the residents of the Keys." She met Bodhi's eyes, "I'd be happy to give you a personal tour of the entire island and all of its buildings, if you're interested, Dr. King."

"Please, call me Bodhi."

She flashed a dazzling smile. " Only if you call me Cleo."

"It's a deal."

Beside him, Detective Williams snorted softly. Then she changed the subject from the amenities available to residents of Golden Shores to the deaths that had plagued it.

"We've just come from the Medical Examiner's Office. He's finishing up the autopsy of Mr. Garcia."

At the mention of the dead man—or perhaps the autopsy itself—Cleo paled slightly under her tan. "Oh?"

"Yes. And according to Dr. Ashland, Mr. Garcia died in a very similar manner to the other cases. No obvious signs of trauma or physical evidence to suggest that death was anything other than the result of natural causes, except of course for the rictus grin," Bodhi explained.

"Rictus grin. So that's the official name for that death mask of horror," she said in a soft voice more to herself than to them.

"Yes. And from what I know so far, I'd say you definitely have a SUD cluster."

"SUD?" she repeated blankly.

"Sudden unexpected death."

"Oh, yes. Well, as I said we're very glad you're here. You seem to be the preeminent expert in clusters of, um, SUD. It would be helpful for me to know what I can do to support you in your efforts." She was all pleasant business again, slipping into her efficient, charming armor as effortlessly as Detective Williams slipped into her cold, brisk armor.

Cleo stopped and waved an identification card in front of a reader, and a pair of gleaming golden doors swung open slowly.

As they stepped into the cool, brightly lit lobby, Bodhi said, "Why don't I start by explaining the best practice for investigating a SUD cluster."

"Wait—is there a definition of a cluster?" Cleo asked.

It was an insightful question—particularly coming from a layperson.

"The particular parameters will vary among researchers, but a cluster refers to some number of deaths that are close in time and space and have no apparent explanation."

"Exactly what we have here," Detective Williams noted.

"Right. And I'm guessing once Dr. Ashland mentioned the possibility of a death cluster, my name came up." The phenomenon was sufficiently rare that an internet search would have led straight to him.

"Yes," Cleo confirmed. Detective Williams nodded her agreement.

"So my recommendation is to undertake a field investigation to uncover commonalities among the deceased. In this case, I'll interview the other residents and your staff members to find out if all the dead had the same dietary habits or engaged in the same hobby. Had they all been exposed to the same viral or bacterial pathogen? Or maybe they were physically intimate with one another. These are just examples, of course. But by asking the right questions, a pattern will emerge."

Cleo gave a small, nervous laugh. "Our guests are adults. So if they choose to be physically intimate, that's their own business. It's not the sort of thing we would track."

"I understand. But they're adults living in close proximity. I imagine much like a college dormitory, there will be whispers up and down the hall. If there were any relationships among the deceased, someone will know."

"Maybe," she allowed.

"Actually, I've been told that Mr. Garcia and Esmeralda Morales were romantically involved," Detective Williams offered.

"Really?"

Cleo seemed mildly surprised that she wasn't already privy to this morsel of gossip but not particularly surprised, either.

"That's what I've heard," Detective Williams

repeated without divulging any details about the information or how she came to possess it.

"Hmm. That may well be, but I can assure you that all five of them were not involved with one another. While I'm not naïve enough to think that none of our guests are sexually active, we are a church-affiliated center. It's not exactly a place where swinging singles would choose to live out their golden years."

It seemed important to move her off the subject of amorous entanglements among the residents. "Again, that's just one example. It may also turn out that the SUD cluster wasn't caused by an environmental condition, but by a shared genetic mutation specific to the ethnicity of the dead."

"The deceased were all Cuban-Americans," Detective Williams reminded them.

"I checked our demographic data. Cuban-Americans make up just under thirty percent of our guests, across our properties. Another ten percent are either African-American or Afro-Cuban. We have a handful of Asian-Americans. And the rest are white."

"Do those percentages hold specifically in the assisted living facility?" Bodhi asked.

Cleo thought for a moment. "More or less. Given

the percentages, would you expect to see some other races dying if it weren't a genetic thing?" she asked.

"I can't say either way just yet. The pathology results should be helpful in teasing out any genetic conditions, though." Then he had a thought. "Although I would like to review whatever medical records you have for the dead to see if they've had any past health concerns in common."

Cleo scrunched up her nose while she considered the request. "I suppose I could let you see them here on site. There would be privacy issues if I let you take them out of the building."

"Sure, that's fine," he assured her.

She uncapped her pen and wrote a note to herself in flowing script in a small notebook she produced from her pocket.

"I'll pull their intake records and any updates to the files that may have come from our in-house medical team. Now, about these interviews you want to do with guests and employees." She paused to choose her words. "I'd like you take into account the fact that people are pretty shaken up. You'll approach this delicately, right?"

Detective Williams let out another muffled snort, which had the effect of drawing Cleo's attention.

"Did you have an idea to contribute, detective?" she asked in a slightly too-sweet voice.

"I'm not sure how to kid glove the fact that people are paying good money to die here," Detective Williams shot back. Her voice echoed off the white marble walls.

Cleo glanced worriedly around the empty lobby.

Before she could shush Detective Williams, the detective went on in a slightly less loud voice. "I want to talk to the employees before they meet with Dr. King."

"Why?"

"If this turns into a criminal investigation, I want the first crack at persons of interest. And since I've asked for, and haven't received, the results of background checks you've done on people you employ, I'm going to have to preemptively consider everyone a person of interest." Her voice was hard.

"I'm pulling that information together. I just need a few more days. I've been busy getting you the scheduling information you wanted," the director answered in an icy voice of her own.

"Does that mean you have it?"

"Certainly. Unlike most hospitals, we don't really rotate staff between daytime and nighttime schedules. So the same six nurses and twelve aides are always scheduled for the evening and overnight shifts. All eighteen employees have been working on at least one night when a guest has passed away."

Anticipating Detective Williams's next question, she consulted her notebook and continued, "And of the eighteen, only three have been present during all the deaths—Nurse Eduardo Martinez and two aides, Philomena Pearl and Charlene Rivers."

Detective Williams's face was unreadable but there was a warning in her voice. "Nobody talks to those three until I'm finished with them."

CHAPTER TWELVE

Felicia excused herself from the conversation with Bodhi and Floridian Barbie and raced up the nearest stairwell to the second floor, where the nursing supervisor sat. Her heart banged in her chest, but when she skidded to a stop in front of the glass-walled office, she willed herself to speak calmly.

"Excuse me," she said, craning her neck to peek inside the office.

The supervisor on duty swiveled around in her chair slowly to look at her.

Great. Felicia suppressed a groan. Jenny Mumma. Or, as the kids at school had called her, Jenny Moo-moo. Jenny was slow and plodding. Thorough. Which in itself wasn't a bad thing, but there was just something bovine about her large brown eyes, as though she were secretly thinking about cud.

Rationally, Felicia knew Jenny hadn't risen to her position as charge nurse by being stupid or ineffective, but she still wished she'd found someone—anyone—else sitting behind the desk. Because she had an urgent situation on her hands, and Jenny wasn't the type to jump.

"What do you need, Felicia?" Jenny said in her slow drawl, which did nothing to detract from the impression that she was lazy.

"I need to know if Eduardo is scheduled to work tonight."

Unfazed by the urgency in Felicia's voice, Jenny methodically sifted through the documents on her desk until she found a schedule book. She paged through it one sheet at a time. Finally, she stopped turning the pages and stared down at a grid in silence.

To keep from screaming for Jenny to hurry up, Felicia fisted her hands and dug her fingernails into her palms. She breathed through her nose.

After an interminable delay, Jenny looked up. "Yep, Nurse Martinez is scheduled to work the six to six shift." She swiveled her head toward the clock hanging in the hallway and then back to Felicia with a languid motion. "He won't be here for another two hours or so," she added as if Felicia couldn't tell time.

"Thanks, Jenny."

She raced away from the office and ducked into the first empty room she found. She whipped out her cell phone, pulled up her contact list, and tapped out a quick text telling Ed she needed to speak to him ASAP. Then she stowed her phone back in her pocket and just stood there, feeling defeated and useless.

She knew Ed wasn't responsible for anyone's death. She knew it as a detective. And she knew it as a friend. But she also knew that right now all signs pointed to Ed, and there was a good chance he'd be blamed—whether that meant he'd be fired, sued, or arrested, she didn't know. She just knew she had to help him.

Adrenaline rushed through her nervous system, making it hard for her to think.

Stay cool, she ordered herself. The way to help Ed was to rule him out as a suspect. Until she could speak to him, she'd have to work on ruling someone else in as a suspect.

She unfolded the sheet of notepaper that Cleo Clarkson had given her and read the names written in Cleo's perfect penmanship. In addition to Ed's name, she'd identified Philomena Pearl and Charlene Rivers. The aides. She'd start there.

The act of devising a plan stilled the anxiety that swirled in her stomach and propelled her forward with purpose.

She strode back to Jenny's office and waited while Jenny painstakingly filled out some form.

After taking a few moments to review her handiwork, Jenny looked up. "You need something else, Felicia?"

"Well, Nurse Mumma," Felicia said in her friendliest voice, "I'm wondering if you could tell me anything about two of the aides who work the overnight shift?"

"I'm sure I could."

"Great. I'm interested in Philomena Pearl and Charlene Rivers."

Something close to alertness or interest sparked in Jenny's indolent eyes. "Oh, the true believers. They're both scheduled to work tonight, too."

"Sorry, did you say true believers?"

Jenny chortled. "Philomena and Charlene work the overnight shift a couple times a week. They're devout followers of Pastor Scott."

"How devout?"

Jenny pulled a face. "Devout enough that they think they're going to strike it rich scrubbing the toilets, swabbing the floors, and bringing people juice because of his Midas touch." She didn't bother to conceal her disdain.

"Are they good workers?" Felicia asked, trying to make sense of the sneer in Jenny's voice. Jenny wasn't the type to look down on someone earning an honest living.

"Well, they're diligent. This place is gleaming when they're done. I'll give them that. But that's only part of their job. They're also supposed to assist the nurses and keep the guests comfortable, which usually means keeping them company if they want to talk or play cards or something. But ..." she trailed off with an uncomfortable look.

"But what?"

"Well, it's... It's just that they make folks uncomfortable."

"Folks? You mean the residents or the nurses?"

"Both. Those two are always proselytizing. It's almost like they get a finder's fee if they convert people to that religion of theirs. They're always going on about financial blessings and honoring God by doing well .... Look, Felicia, it's just weird. Philomena drives a fancy convertible. Charlene's always dripping in jewelry. I don't know where they get their money, but they're tacky about it."

Felicia scribbled a note to herself. "Interesting. Thanks."

The nurse pinkened and hurriedly added, "But I'm not saying they're bad people or bad workers."

"It's okay, Jenny. This wasn't an official interview. I'm not putting any of that into my notes."

Jenny exhaled and rolled her shoulders. "That's a relief."

"But I want you to do me a favor."

"Depends. What is it?"

"Point me in their direction when they show up for work tonight if I'm still here."

"I suppose I could do that."

CHAPTER THIRTEEN

Bodhi gazed around the enormous kitchen, deliberately keeping his mouth closed to stop from gaping. He recognized that his culinary tastes tended toward the simple, possibly even the ascetic. So he knew he didn't appropriately appreciate the room. But even he could see the kitchen would have been more fitting for a Michelin-starred restaurant—or perhaps, more accurately, the set of a cooking show—than a medium-sized assisted living facility.

Two large islands anchored the room—one made of highly polished, pure white marble, the other of highly burnished copper. The six-burner cooktop, also copper, was the largest he'd ever seen. The wide vent hood was copper; and all the pots and pans hanging from ceiling were copper, as were the enormous refrigerator, the two dishwashers, and the deep double sink.

The light bounced off the metal and the snowy white cabinetry, creating a blinding, prismatic effect.

Chef Pedro Tonga watched him. "It's a lot to take in," the chef said.

"I'll say. Have you ever worked in a kitchen like this before?" Bodhi waved his hands in the air.

"No. And I did stints at the White House and a Four Seasons property. This is... well, excessive."

"What's with all the copper? Is it good for cooking?"

The chef followed his gaze to the pots and pans dangling above them. "Eh, it's okay. Personally, I prefer cast-iron. But the church, they wanted gold everything. Gold is useless in the kitchen. So, we compromised. They get their pretty copper. I get something that I can work with."

"All the copper's an effort to communicate prosperity, then?"

The chef shrugged. "Beats me. I don't involve myself in their religion. And they don't involve themselves in my menu."

"So you set the menu independently, then?" Bodhi confirmed.

A shadow crossed Chef Tonga's face. "Yes, mainly. With some caveats."

"For example?" Bodhi prompted in a neutral voice.

The chef made an irritated gesture. "For example, the people I'm feeding are old. They need to be eating a plant-based diet. Actually, we all do."

"I agree."

"Yes, meat should be a garnish or a side. But Pastor Scott wants everyone to feel rich by eating rich food. So, yes, I set the menu, but I do have to find a way to serve filet mignon, lump crabmeat, and lobster. And he likes me to add rich sauces and thick glazes. He wants everyone to indulge in chocolate this and caramel that."

"So you *don't* have final say over your menu?"

"I submit my proposed weekly menu. He marks it up with suggestions. I reject the most extravagant and send it back. And we go back and forth like that. We always end up with a menu that's about eighty percent nutritious and twenty percent indulgent."

"Moderation in all things, including moderation, eh?"

"That's the saying." Chef Tonga laughed.

"I assume some of the residents have dietary restrictions. How do you deal with those?"

The chef motioned with his left hand. "Come with me."

Bodhi followed him to a marble workspace that held an iPad and several glossy white binders.

The chef woke up the device then touched an icon on the screen. A list of names appeared.

"These are my guests who have requirements that need to be met for medical reasons. I have menus for each of the restricted diets—low sodium, low fat, what have you—in these binders. All of our guests choose from among three options at each meal. If the choices don't comport with a guest's diet, we give that guest three other options to choose from. I believe people deserve to have choices."

"Could I get a list of people with dietary restrictions?

The chef thought for a moment. Then he shrugged. "I don't see why not."

He tapped the printer icon, and a machine whirred to life somewhere nearby. Chef Tonga retrieved the printout and handed it to Bodhi just as Cleo Clarkson peered through the doorway.

"Pardon the interruption, chef. Dr. King, are you almost finished talking to Chef Tonga?"

Bodhi nodded. "I may have more questions later, but for now I think I have what I need."

He thanked the chef for his time then followed Cleo out into the hallway.

"Are you okay?" Bodhi asked.

Cleo eyed the forensic pathologist nervously. "Why do you ask?"

He held her gaze levelly. "I don't know you very well. Or at all, really. But you seem to be upset about something."

Cleo's pulse fluttered in her throat. He was right, of course. She was upset. But she didn't quite know how to put her worry into words with a stranger, so she pushed it to the side. "I'm just fine, thank you. I wanted to let you know I've gathered all of the medical files you needed," she said smoothly.

He looked at her for another moment then said, "Oh, okay."

For an instant, she felt stupid for interrupting him on such a thin pretense, but she reminded herself that she was the director. She was just being efficient by tracking him down in the kitchen—even though they both knew the files could have waited.

She made a small noise in her throat. "Why don't I show you to the library?"

"Lead the way."

He grinned at her, and she felt her own mouth curve into a smile in response.

As he followed her up the two flights of stairs, she

explained, "I reserved a library carrel for you. I'm sorry we don't have a spare office you can use, but if you need anything at all, just let the librarian know. He'll call me."

"I'm sure the library will be perfectly adequate."

She led him along the hallway and into the Golden Reading Room. She heard his intake of breath and knew that he found the library to be far more than adequate.

She could relate. Of all the opulent spaces in the building, the library was quite possibly the most impressive. She could still remember the first time she walked into it. The Tiffany lights over the deeply polished mahogany and cherry tables. The floor-to-ceiling windows. The rich brocade wallpaper peeking out here and there between the soaring bookshelves. The twin spiral staircases that seemed to reach to the heavens and the catwalks that led to the upper shelves.

Anyone who'd ever held a book and inhaled its heady leather and paper scent would fall in love with the space. She smiled and watched his face.

"Wow," he breathed.

"It's breathtaking, isn't it? I feel that way every time I walk in here. Let me show you where I've set you up."

She led him across the thick claret carpet that

silenced their steps to the barest hush of a whisper. His files were in the carrel across from Lynette Johnson's favorite spot. She figured the retired attorney would get a kick out of questioning the forensic consultant when she wandered down to the library for her nightly visit.

Bodhi King surveyed the neat stacks of folders, the collection of pens, and the pile of fresh legal pads she'd set out for him. A copper reading lamp cast a warm glow over the materials. A chilled bottle of water sat on a tile coaster.

She flipped a panel on the right carrel wall to reveal a charging station. "Just in case you need to charge your phone or any devices while you're here."

"Thanks so much, Cleo. I think I've got everything I need."

"Good. I'm still working on arranging the guest interviews. As you asked, I'm starting with their closest friends. But I will need to run all the interviews by Pastor Scott and his board. I'm sure you understand," she added apologetically.

He made a noncommittal sound.

"Well, then, I'll leave you to it. I'll check back on you in a bit."

She began to walk away. Then, almost against her own volition, she turned back.

"Bodhi?" she called softly from several feet away.

He looked up at her, his palm on the unopened folder on the top of the stack.

"Yes?"

Somehow, she felt as though he was the first person who had ever truly seen her. The real her, not just her physicality.

Shaking off the disorientating feeling, she took a breath and plowed forward, "I was wondering if I could buy you a drink later tonight—when we're finished here?" she asked in a forced casual voice.

He smiled gently. "I don't drink."

"Oh. I just thought we could talk." Hot blood rushed to her face.

He continued as though she hadn't said anything, "Detective Williams and I are meeting Dr. Ashland at a place called Mangrove Mama's later. That sounds like the sort of place where you could have a drink and we could have a chat. Is that convenient for you?"

A rush of relief replaced her embarrassment. "Sure. I know Mangrove Mama's. It's on Sugarloaf Key. I can meet you there."

"Great. I may need a lift to wherever I'm staying after."

"Where are you staying?" she asked, her curiosity getting the better of her.

"Good question. I'll have to ask Detective Williams." He smiled again and waited for her to turn away before returning his attention to the folder.

She trotted out of the library on shaky legs and ran straight into Mr. Santiago on his way in.

"Cleo," Hector greeted her heartily. "You're flushed."

"Am I?" She asked breathlessly.

He eyed her wordlessly.

She gave a self-conscious laugh. "I'm a little flustered. What are you doing here? Returning your book already?"

He nodded. "I finished it sooner than I thought I would. Interesting guy. He was a good general. Kind of an unpleasant man, though." He tapped the cover. "I'm thinking magical realism for my bedtime reading."

"You can't go wrong with Isabel Allende."

Mr. Santiago nodded approvingly. "As always, you're a woman of impeccable tastes."

She smiled. "Good night, Mr. Santiago."

His expression grew serious. "I hope so, dear. I hope it's a good night for all of us."

"So do I, Mr. Santiago. So do I."

CHAPTER FOURTEEN

Arthur stuck his head into his grandmother's room and knocked gently on the frame of the open door.

She looked up from her crossword puzzle and blinked at him.

"Arturo, I didn't expect to see you until this weekend. Is something wrong? Are you preaching again?" Her hand fluttered to her throat.

He hurried across the room and kissed her forehead. "No, *lita*. Everything's fine. I just thought I'd come and see you again before our Sunday dinner."

She patted his hand. "What a nice surprise."

He dragged a chair from the other side of the room so he could sit across from her. Then he opened his messenger bag and removed the plastic shopping bag from the botanica. He unwrapped the Ajo Macho candle and handed it to her. "Also, I wanted to give you this."

Tears of relief shone in her eyes and she took the candle with trembling hands. She muttered something in rapid Spanish. It sounded like a prayer of thanksgiving.

"You got the dressing and oils, too?"

He nodded and placed them on the table between them.

She examined the items in silence then exhaled loudly. "This is good." She pointed toward the jewelry box that sat on top of her dresser against the far wall. "Will you please get my lighter? Your grandfather's Zippo. It's under my necklaces."

He crossed the room and rooted through her collection of seldom-worn jewelry until he found the lighter with her second husband's initials engraved in the silver case.

"Do you want me to light it for you?"

She followed his gaze to her still trembling hands and laughed. "Ah, I'm just excited. It's not time to light it yet. I need to prepare it."

"Oh. Do you want me to help?"

Her shrewd eyes met his. She shook her head slowly. "No. You're not a true believer. I need to set my intentions and anoint the candle while I'm focused. You and your church doctrine will be a distraction."

He suppressed a frown—not because she was disparaging the Golden Island Church, but because he needed to know how to prepare his own candle. He'd hoped to learn what steps to take by watching her. But he had to respect her wishes, especially knowing that he was going to be preaching to her and her friends about the presence of Satan again in the days to come.

"Okay. Should I leave you?"

"Please. I want to get this ready before darkness falls and the evil spirits start to prowl the halls." Her eyes dared him to challenge her superstition.

"I understand, *lita.*" He kissed her cheek and stood to leave. "I'll see you this weekend."

"Arturo?" she called as he stepped out of the room.

He turned back. "Yes?"

"Thank you. I know I might seem like a silly old lady to you—"

"Please don't. Whatever brings you peace. I just wish you could commit yourself to the abundant blessings that come from Pastor Scott's gospel and not this ... magic ritual."

She sighed. "Good night, Arthur."

"Good night. Will I see you at the Spread the Word lay ministry meeting on Sunday?"

"Oh, honey, no. I'll be at Father Rafael's Mass. Stop by after you're all done ministering, though. We can play cards until dinner."

He felt his shoulders slumping toward the ground. He nodded and left the room, pulling the door most of the way shut behind him.

CHAPTER FIFTEEN

Bodhi laced his fingers together behind his head and tipped the heavy chair back on two legs so he could stare up through the skylight at the cloudless sapphire sky. He allowed his gaze to fall on the prisms of light reflecting on the glass as he reviewed what he'd learned from the stack of medical records at his elbow.

As was to be expected, the recently deceased residents of Golden Shores had suffered from an array of chronic ailments ranging from arthritis to diabetes to asthma. Mr. Garcia had been allergic to penicillin and had had both knees replaced. Ms. Morales had had two fairly recent broken wrists and a fairly old breast lumpectomy. Mr. Gonzales had had high cholesterol and high blood pressure. The list of conditions went on, but there was no common thread among the dead. He'd read every file cover to cover twice. The answer wasn't on paper.

"Well, if you're not the picture of a man lost in thought, I don't know what is."

He looked around for the amused voice and eventually surmised that it belonged to the woman peering over the carrel's shared wall.

"Hi there. I must not have heard you come in," he said.

The carrel was in a quiet corner, set away from both the circulation desk and the popular fiction room. As a result, he'd been immersed in his reading, undistracted by traffic or chatter.

She gave him a mischievous grin. "I'll say. Been here for about half an hour. You haven't looked up so much as once. I was wishing I'd brought my whoopie cushion with me. I could've sat on that and got your attention."

He laughed then stood and reached across the divider. "I'm Bodhi King."

She took his hand. Her skin was cool and soft. Her grip was surprisingly strong. "Lynette Johnson, retired defense attorney and general ne'er-do-well."

He couldn't help but laugh. "It's nice to meet you, Mrs. Johnson."

"Please. They only call me Mrs. Johnson around here when I'm in trouble. Lynette will do just fine." She released his hand. "So you're the forensics expert."

It sounded more like a statement than a question. He gave her a close look.

"Did my reputation precede me?"

"No, just the fact of your existence. But now that I've got a name, I'll be sure to look you up and find out all about you," she promised.

"Let me save you some time. I'm a retired forensic pathologist, formerly with the Allegheny County Coroner's Office—"

"You don't look old enough to be retired."

"Yet, I am."

One perfectly groomed eyebrow shot up Lynette's forehead. "Sounds like there's a story behind that."

"There is, but it's a long one."

"I've got nowhere to be."

He laughed. "The short version is I uncovered a death cluster in Pittsburgh. It developed into a local political scandal. Throw in some corporate malfeasance, an adulterous affair, and an unfortunate office rivalry that ended with my kidnapping, and, well, as you might imagine, the press covered it pretty heavily."

"I'll bet," she said drily.

"The attention got to be a bit much for me. So,

after the cases wrapped up, I took an extended sabbatical. And, I just never went back to the coroner's office."

She studied his face. "But you figured out what caused the deaths?"

She focused on the salient detail from the story like any good trial attorney would.

"That's right."

Interest sparked in her eyes. "Well? What was it?"

"Five otherwise healthy females in their late teens and early twenties died suddenly, in most cases after reporting feeling feverish and fatigued. The cause of death was myocarditis, an infection of the heart."

"Did they catch it from one another?"

"No. It's not contagious."

"Then how ...?"

"It turned out that they all had been drinking a sports energy beverage that contained wild red ginseng that hadn't been properly sourced."

"Ginseng caused a deadly heart infection?"

"It's a little more complicated than that. The ginseng in question had been contaminated. And the women who died all had low body fat. Those factors and the fact that carbonation intensifies the effects of certain herbs all interacted and resulted in the deaths."

Lynette processed this information then gave him

a skeptical look. "So you think all the folks who've died here ingested the same thing, and that's what killed them?"

"Possibly. Or they were all exposed to the same airborne pathogen. Or they all swam in the same water. Some common thread exists. And then, just as with the cases in Pittsburgh, the dead may have shared some underlying physical characteristic or condition that also contributed."

"Hmm."

She still didn't seem convinced. He smiled reassuringly.

"I suppose I'd better let you get back to it."

"Wait," he said before she disappeared behind the divider. "Do you know if there's a computer here I could use to access electronic databases?"

"Sure. There's a computer room behind the magazine area. I log on every week to keep up with developments in caselaw. What do you need?"

"Just an internet connection. I can log in to the medical journal databases as long as I can get online."

"Sure. I'll show you where the computers are."

He followed her out of the room and down a short hallway. She stopped in front a glass-walled room. Inside, four computers sat two by two on two long tables. "This is it. I sure hope you find what you're looking for. And fast." Her wide smile wobbled.

Me, too, he thought. *Me, too.*

CHAPTER SIXTEEN

Conquer anger with non-anger.

THE BUDDHA,
DHAMMAPADA

Be angry, and do not sin.
Meditate within your heart on your
bed, and be still.

PSALM 4:4

Felicia knew she was in a foul temper, and she knew she was taking her irritation out on Bodhi. But she couldn't seem to help herself.

When Ed had finally gotten back to her, she'd been unable to convince him that the situation was serious. The more she'd tried to explain that he needed to find a good criminal defense attorney and then lawyer up, the more he'd insisted he'd done nothing wrong. It didn't matter how many times she told him the facts didn't matter as much as how things looked, she couldn't seem to get through to him.

As soon as she filed a report containing the fact that Eduardo Martinez was the only nurse who'd been working during all five deaths, the chief would order her to bring him in for questioning. And the smart money was on the district attorney deciding to charge him, even if there wasn't evidence that he was culpable.

Gossip about the deaths at Golden Shores was spreading through the Keys like pink eye through a kindergarten classroom. The politicians who'd handed Bryce Scott and his church a big, juicy tax break when they'd bought the island now wanted to shut down the news about folks dying at the assisted care facility. She didn't think they'd be particularly concerned about whether Ed was actually responsible for the deaths. But Ed had just laughed her off.

Her mood hadn't improved when Jenny Mumma flagged her down to let her know Philomena Pearl and Charlene Rivers had both called off work to attend some church function. According to Jenny, Golden

Shores' policy was extremely liberal with regard to permitting personal time for Golden Island Church activities, and there was nothing she could do to compel the aides to show up for their shift.

So, having spent the entire afternoon and most of the evening at Golden Shores with absolutely nothing to show for it, Felicia had been irate to learn that Bodhi had invited Cleo to meet them at the bar.

"That woman should be working around the clock trying to figure out why her guests are dropping dead. She has no business going out for drinks," Felicia grumbled as they disembarked from the yacht and made their way across the parking lot.

"I'm sorry. I didn't realize it would upset you if she joined us. But she's not coming until later. She said it would be close to ten o'clock by the time she gets there. We'll have plenty of time to bring Dr. Ashland up to date and learn whether he has anything for us before she shows up." Bodhi's tone was apologetic but carried a hint of confusion, as if he wasn't quite sure what her problem was.

Neither was she.

She gritted her teeth and walked faster. By treating her as if she were being reasonable, he was just making her feel more unreasonable.

After a while she said, "I'm not upset, I'm tired.

And I'm frustrated because I didn't get to interview the aides. That's all."

He nodded but said nothing.

She popped the locks on the sedan and slid behind the wheel, slamming the door harder than was necessary. He took his time getting in on the passenger side. She tried to use the moment alone to calm down. But her heart was hammering, and the anger in her gut was roiling.

When he finally sat down beside her, he gave her a long look. Then he said mildly, "Detective Williams, you might find it more helpful to acknowledge your feelings without judgment and then let them pass than to try to deny them."

She shot him a suspicious sidelong look. "How?"

"Like this. Take a breath and notice that you're angry."

She rolled her eyes, but inhaled. She felt the hot flare in her belly, quickly followed by a clawing shame at her lack of control. "Now what?"

"Now, instead of judging your anger, just acknowledge it. Say to yourself—or aloud—I'm angry."

"I'm angry," she growled.

"Great. Now, having named your emotion, let it go."

"What does that mean, let it go?" She was willing

to try his stupid idea, but not if he was going to hide behind meaningless mumbo-jumbo.

"It means you let the fact that you're angry pass through you. It doesn't mean your anger will magically dissipate. It just means, you accept it as an emotion and move on."

Fine. She was angry.

"And then what do I do?"

"Nothing. Just note your anger as a mildly interesting piece of information and then forget about it."

"You're telling me that just by knowing I'm angry, I'll be less angry?"

He met her gaze with clear, untroubled eyes. "There's no harm in trying it, is there?"

She narrowed her eyes and didn't answer. She took another deep breath and made note of the red hot feeling that filled her. Then she told herself, 'Okay. You're pissed.'

When her brain started to chide her for her loss of control, she batted the thought away. Her heart rate lowered a notch. Her breathing slowed. The grip of her emotion loosened.

She turned and gave Bodhi a wide-eyed look. What kind of Buddhist magic was this?

"That's it? That's all I have to do to find inner peace?" she demanded.

He smiled. "No. But it's a start."

She turned the key in the ignition to start the car. "I'm sorry I was snappish."

He said nothing but gave her an encouraging nod.

"I'm worried about a friend." The words flew out of her mouth before she realized she'd said them.

"Oh?"

His tone suggested he'd listen to whatever she wanted to tell him, but he wasn't going to pry. Playing true confessions wasn't really her style, but why not? They had a twenty-minute drive to Sugarloaf Key.

"Yeah. A guy I grew up with—Eduardo Martinez."

"The nurse who was working during all five deaths?"

"Right. Ed's a good guy. There's no way he's involved in anything—"

"Hang on. There's no evidence *anyone's* implicated in the deaths, Detective. That's why I'm here, isn't it? To find an explanation."

She made an impatient gesture with her right hand. "Sure, right. Maybe there's no forensic evidence —yet. But you'd have to be naive to think that the district attorney and my chief aren't going to take one look at the fact that Ed was there and make him their number one suspect. The community wants closure, an answer. They're not going to worry too much about the details—believe me."

"You think your friend will be railroaded in the absence of another explanation?"

She did.

"I do." Her stomach tightened as she said the words.

"Hmmm."

"What?"

"I suppose we'll just have to keep doing what we're doing—search for a genuine explanation for the death cluster."

His sanguine attitude would have come across as patronizing from just about anybody else. But, from Bodhi King, it was a comfort. She clung to it.

"I hope so."

He rested his hand, briefly, just for a second or two, on her forearm.

"I'll find the medical answer. You keep gathering facts and interviewing witnesses. Your friend will be okay."

"I hope so," she breathed. Then after a moment, she said, "I wanted to talk to those two aides tonight ..."

"But?"

"But they called off. Neither of them came in for their shift."

"They both called off? That's interesting."

Again with the mild tone.

She shrugged. "The nursing supervisor seemed to think it wasn't all that unusual. They're members of Scott's church, and there was some sort of meeting or event."

"Oh?"

"Spit it out, Bodhi."

She didn't know if his attempts to gently lead her to some point of view were a Buddhist thing or a doctor thing, but, either way, she didn't have the patience for it.

"I don't claim to be an expert on Christianity, but most organizations—religious or otherwise—schedule meetings and events pretty far in advance."

"Christians included," she confirmed.

"So, if this was a regularly planned meeting, those women presumably could have requested the night off in advance."

"Okay. But maybe it was an emergency meeting or something."

"Maybe."

"You're saying the timing is suspicious," she pressed him.

"If not suspicious, it's at least convenient."

She fell silent. He was right. Whether Jenny

Mumma saw anything out of the ordinary about Philomena Pearl and Charlene Rivers's last-minute absence, it did warrant further investigation.

And it gave her an excuse to circumvent Cleo Clarkson and go straight to Bryce Scott. A shiver of anticipation zipped up her spine at the thought of finally pinning down the church leader and getting some solid answers.

"Thanks."

He wrinkled his brow. "I didn't do anything."

"Oh, you did," she informed him gleefully.

She switched on the radio and let Jimmy Buffet serenade them the rest of the way to Sugarloaf Key.

CHAPTER SEVENTEEN

J oel Ashland raised his beer bottle in greeting, then waved Bodhi and Detective Williams over to his table, which was tucked into a corner behind the bar.

The steel drum band playing out on the patio was loud, and the happy hour revelers singing along were louder still, but when Bodhi reached the medical examiner's table, the noise faded, as if it were being carried out to the ocean by the wind.

"I see you got your favorite table," Detective Williams commented.

"I know the right people." Dr. Ashland winked and gestured for them to sit.

A waitress hurried over to take their drink orders. "Sorry, Felicia, but you and your friend missed happy hour. The specials ended an hour ago."

"No sweat, Stacey. I'll just have a Landshark."

Stacey smiled at Bodhi. "And your friend?"

"A club soda, please."

"You want a lime with that?"

"Sure. Thanks."

She stowed her pen behind her ear and walked over to the bar to get the drinks. The lead singer announced the band was going on break. Detective Williams slid a laminated menu across the table to Bodhi.

"You might as well order something. The fridge where you're staying isn't stocked," she told him.

"Where *am* I staying?"

She exchanged glances and with the medical examiner. Then she turned to Bodhi. "Well, seeing as how you didn't want to take the church up on their offer to cover your expenses, it's not going to be a guest villa on Golden Island. The medical examiner's office is going to put you up."

Dr. Ashland nodded. "It's tough to get a room on short notice—even out of season, so you can stay at my place. It's just across the road."

"At the campground?" Bodhi had noticed the sign on the drive down from Big Pine Key.

"Yeah. I have a vintage Airstream—you know, the silver campers. It's got plenty of room for two. And it has a kitchen, but as Felicia noted, the cupboards are bare."

Bodhi scanned the menu and found a black bean sandwich. Then he leaned forward, "So you live in the camper?"

Just then, the waitress returned with Detective Williams's beer and his club soda. She overheard the question and laughed. "Oh, that's just temporary. Until he finds a place, right, Doc?"

Detective Williams took a swig of beer then joined Stacey in laughter.

"That's right," Dr. Ashland confirmed.

"He's been temporarily living in that thing for four years," Detective Williams explained.

Dr. Ashland shrugged. "I kind of like it. I have a nice view of the water. Nobody bothers me there. And I don't have to mess around with mowing a lawn or paying a homeowner's association some sort of maintenance fee."

"And he can stumble across the street when this place closes for the night," Stacey added.

"It sounds great," Bodhi told him. "Thanks for putting me up."

Detective Williams rolled her eyes.

Stacey muttered, "Men." She took their food

orders and promised the kitchen would have their meals out quickly.

After she left, Detective Williams turned to Dr. Ashland with an expectant look.

"Well? Did you figure out what killed Carlos Garcia?"

"Sure."

"And?"

"His heart stopped beating," he said acidly.

The humor was lost on Detective Williams, who let out her breath in a loud whoosh of disappointment.

Dr. Ashland turned to Bodhi. "What about you two? Did you learn anything at Golden Shores?"

Bodhi could tell from the way Detective Williams tensed her shoulders, as if she were bracing for a blow, that she thought he was going to bring up Nurse Martinez. It wasn't his place to speculate on the suspect list, though.

Instead he said, "I met with Ms. Clarkson to discuss the contours of the field investigation."

"I'd like to discuss Ms. Clarkson's contours," Dr. Ashland laughed.

Detective Williams shot him a look of pure disgust.

Bodhi went on as though he hadn't heard the double entendre. "She provided me with the medical records for the five deceased individuals and is going to set up a time for me to interview residents and staff—after Detective Williams has had a chance to question them."

Dr. Ashland blinked at him. "You reviewed all their records? Did anything jump out at you?"

"Not really," Bodhi admitted. "I had to read them there—patient privacy rules, But I took my time going over them. I didn't see anything that could explain the death cluster."

The medical examiner slumped in his chair. Detective Williams glared at her beer as though the beverage were responsible for the news.

"Great," she muttered. "Now what?"

"I do have a theory," Bodhi ventured.

Dr. Ashland leaned forward, and Detective Williams's eyes lit with interest.

"But it's very preliminary," he warned. "And we'll need to have a lab do a DNA analysis to confirm it."

Dr. Ashland cocked his head to the side. "You're thinking a genetic mutation may be responsible?"

"Maybe. After I finished reviewing the medical records, I got online at Golden Shores' library and accessed the journal databases. I searched for mentions of the rictus grin in the literature."

"And?" Detective Williams prompted.

"And, in addition to cases of tetanus and strychnine poisoning, *risus sardonicus* has been seen in cases where the deceased suffered from Wilson disease."

"Wilson disease," Dr. Ashland mused.

"Who's Wilson? And what's the disease?" Detective Williams wanted to know.

Bodhi shrugged. "Presumably the researcher who discovered the condition was named Wilson. Wilson disease is an inherited genetic disorder. In people who have the mutation, excessive copper accumulates in their bodies—mainly in the liver, brain, and eyes."

"And it kills you?" she asked.

"It can, if left untreated. And one symptom of Wilson disease is excessive grinning during life, which can manifest at death as the rictus grin," Bodhi explained.

Dr. Ashland shook his head. "I don't know. Doesn't Wilson disease usually cause liver failure? The deceased all had fairly healthy livers—although I think Ms. Morales liked her cocktails."

Bodhi conceded the point. "Wilson disease typically shows up in teenagers. And, in younger people, it's more likely to cause liver disease. But the literature indicates that liver problems are less likely to manifest when older people are struck by the disease. In that population, psychiatric and neurological problems are more common."

Dr. Ashland glanced at the detective. "Has anyone mentioned any mental issues to you?"

"Things like confusion, depression, anxiety, or pronounced mood swings," Bodhi elaborated.

She shook her head. "Not according to Clarkson. But, the families have said that some of them had been getting forgetful. And after the first two deaths, everybody in that place is scared, confused, and anxious."

"Sure. Can't you interview the residents to get a fuller picture?" Dr. Ashland asked.

"That's on the schedule for tomorrow. Cleo's pulling together a list of residents who were closest to those who died," Bodhi said.

Stacey delivered his sandwich and Dr. Ashland's fish platter. Then she returned with a full rack of ribs, which she placed in front of Detective Williams with a flourish. "Dig in."

The band returned to the stage. Bodhi leaned toward the medical examiner. "Did all the deceased have brown eyes?"

"Mmm-hmm," Dr. Ashland confirmed around a mouthful of grouper. He swallowed and wiped his mouth with his napkin. "And no, before you ask, none of them had the Kayser-Fleischer ring."

"What ring?" Detective Williams asked,

depositing a picked-clean rib bone on her plate delicately.

"The Kayser-Fleischer ring is a greenish-brown ring that can form around the eye from copper deposits. It's pretty common in people with Wilson disease," Bodhi explained.

"So, it's *not* Wilson disease then?"

Dr. Ashland shrugged. "The ring is common, but it's not universal. And ... while I think I'd have noticed it, given the eye color of the deceased, maybe I missed it."

Bodhi knew too well the doubt and unease that was creeping into Joel Ashland's voice.

"Don't second-guess yourself. If there were unusual eye changes, the families would have mentioned it when they saw the bodies."

"Except for the ones who were cremated. And Garcia. His family hasn't flown in," Detective Williams pointed out.

"But still, what are the odds that five unrelated people in one facility would have the same relatively rare genetic disorder? And that none of them showed any signs of it earlier in life?" Dr. Ashland mused.

Bodhi nodded. The medical examiner raised valid points. "In a vacuum, I'd say slim-to-none. But two things to consider—one, the dead all share the same ethnic background. It's conceivable that the mutation is more common in people of Cuban descent than in the general population. And, two, the disease manifests when copper builds up."

"Okay? So?" Detective Williams demanded.

"So, I toured the kitchen at Golden Shores. Guess what every single pot and pan in that place is made of?"

Detective Williams froze with a rib halfway to her mouth. Dr. Ashland put down his beer. They both pinned their eyes on Bodhi.

"Copper?"

"Copper."

CHAPTER EIGHTEEN

Bryce walked into the meeting room with Becki by his side. As they entered, Bryce swept his gaze across the faces of the group seated around the table.

Arthur, Philomena, Charlene, Roger, and Ron looked back at him with smiles that displayed varying degrees of eagerness. Cleo, however, sat alone, with an empty chair on each side, and did not look up when the door opened. Her head was bent over a notebook and she was writing intently.

Bryce stopped and considered the seating arrangement. As was customary, the chair at the head of the table had been left vacant for him.

Instead of taking it, he got Cleo's attention. "Ms. Clarkson, if you don't mind moving down a seat in either direction." He gestured to her left and her right.

She lifted her head and blinked at him. Then she slid her notebook and pen over one space, scooped up her purse, and moved one chair to her left.

He strode to the seat she'd just vacated and sat down. "Becki, right here beside me if you will."

Becki glanced at the empty chair at the head of the table then trotted across the floor to take the spot next to him. Once she had arranged herself and pulled out her iPad to take notes, he poured himself a glass of ice water from the pitcher in the center of the table.

Bryce took a sip of cold water then bowed his head. "Let us pray. Dear Lord, we are gathered here tonight to do your will and to shine your light on the evils lurking in Golden Shores. Please bless us and our efforts and give us the courage and the vision to bring Golden Shores out of this darkness and into a more prosperous and profitable season for us and for you. Amen."

The group assembled around the table murmured 'Amen.'

Bryce lifted his head. "Thank you for being here on such short notice. I've convened a meeting of this group because it's urgent that we make some decisions about Golden Shores. For that reason, I've invited Ms. Clarkson to participate."

Beside him, Becki lifted her pen into the air and gave him a confused look.

"Becki, do you have a question?"

"Yes, I'm afraid I'm not sure which committee this is. I have to apologize—I thought I knew all the standing committees, but I must not." She mumbled the last words as though she were ashamed of herself.

"No need to feel embarrassed, Becki. This isn't one of our standing committees. This is an ad hoc committee, and I should identify all the participants so your notes are accurate. Attending this ad hoc committee to address the troubling situation at Golden Shores are the following individuals: Pastor Bryce Scott, spiritual leader and director of Golden Island church and CEO and president of Golden Shores Living Community, Inc. Also attending is Ms. Cleo Clarkson, director of resident life at Golden Shores Assisted Living Facility; Arthur Lopez, lay minister responsible for the spiritual lives of the residents of Golden Shores; Ron Porter, associate director of lay ministry programs; Roger Howard, representing the church council; Charlene Rivers, a member of the church social outreach committee and an employee of Golden Shores; and Philomena Pearl, religious education assistant leader and also an employee of Golden Shores. That's everyone." He smiled warmly at her.

Becki smiled back and lowered her eyelashes. "Thank you, Pastor Bryce."

"With the formalities out of the way, I've asked you here because the already troubling situation at Golden Shores has gotten worse."

Across the table, Philomena clutched her chest. "Not another death?" Her voice shook.

"No, I am happy to say that since Ms. Morales's unfortunate passage through the Pearly Gates, there have been no more deaths at Golden Shores." He paused a beat. "Unless Ms. Clarkson has something more recent to report," he added acerbically.

Six sets of eyes swiveled to Cleo, who sat back, wide-eyed for a moment. But when she spoke, her voice was neither flustered nor defensive.

"I can confirm that no additional guests have died since Ms. Morales passed away." She turned slightly to her right and gave him a lidded gaze.

At the far end of the table, Roger boomed, "Well, thank the good Lord for small mercies."

A titter of nervous laughter traveled through the room. Bryce waited for it to fade before he went on.

"Despite the fact no one has died in the past two days, there are significant problems at Golden Shores. I'd like to begin by having Ms. Clarkson address the steps she and her staff are taking to correct the situation."

Cleo folded her hands on the table in front of her and took a moment to scan her notebook. Then she lifted her head with a confident half-smile on her lips.

"Thank you, Pastor Scott. Friends, I'm so grateful for the opportunity to share the steps we're taking to ensure the safety of our guests and to conduct a thorough investigation of the recent spate of deaths. The technical term for the situation at Golden Shores, for those of you who are interested, is an SUD cluster."

"I'm sorry," Becki said as she tapped notes into her device. "Did you say suds? Like, soap bubbles?"

Cleo leaned in front of Bryce to answer the question. His attention was drawn to the curve of her neck. He inhaled sharply, and his nostrils flared. She didn't seem to notice.

"Capital *S-U-D*. SUD cluster. SUD stands for sudden unexplained death."

She drew back, and Bryce pulled his eyes away.

"Thanks," Becki stage whispered.

"No problem."

Before continuing, Cleo looked around the table, making eye contact with each person for several seconds before moving onto the next.

"As I was saying, a cluster of five, sudden unexplained deaths is what we've suffered at Golden Shores over the past month. According to our county medical examiner, Dr. Joel Ashland, there's no readily apparent explanation for the sudden deaths of our guests."

Ron interjected, "Doesn't the fact that these deaths are unexplained just mean Doc Ashland doesn't know his rear end from his elbow?"

Although Bryce privately shared Ron's view, he maintained a neutral expression while another wave of chuckles swept the table.

"Actually, Dr. Ashland reached out to an expert in SUD clusters. As some of you may know, there's a retired forensic pathologist from Pennsylvania who has some experience in the area." Cleo's lips smiled, but her eyes didn't.

"That would be Dr. Bodhi King," Bryce elaborated. "Those of you on the board will recall that we approved a consulting offer and submitted it to Dr. King last week."

Charlene Rivers raised a tentative hand. "I'm not on the board, but my Charlie is. He said that doctor from Pennsylvania rejected the offer."

Cleo answered before Bryce could. "That's

correct. Dr. King feels strongly that being retained by the church or the assisted care facility would give the wrong impression. He wants to be sure the community understands his investigation is independent and unbiased. So, although he declined our offer, the police department had also contacted him."

"That's a handy coincidence. He held out for more money, huh?" Roger mused.

"I don't think so. I don't know what budget he has from the police department and the medical examiner's office, but I can't imagine they were more financially generous than we were," Bryce interjected.

"In any event, Dr. King has agreed to do a field study of the death cluster at Golden Shores for the authorities. And we, of course, have committed our full cooperation and assistance," Cleo said.

Arthur coughed. "You keep saying cluster. So this is a cluster of sudden unexplained deaths because they all happened in the same place?"

"That's right. According to Dr. King, a SUD cluster is identified when there's a spate of deaths that are close both geographically and temporally—in place and in time. So given that we've lost five guests in a month, that would be considered a SUD cluster."

Cleo glanced down at her notes and then looked

back up. "I'm happy to answer as many questions as you have. Why don't I just go through my report and you can feel free to raise the questions as they come up?"

Bryce stiffened at her subtle wresting of control of the meeting, but again maintained a blank expression. "Please go on."

"Dr. King arrived today. I showed him around the facility and we talked generally about what his field investigation will entail. The first thing he wanted to do was to review the medical records and health files for the guests who've died."

"Is that a good idea?" Roger asked.

"I'd figured he'd ask to see those, so I'd already consulted our attorneys about the issue. On advice of counsel, I gave him access to the files to review, but informed him they were not to leave the premises. He spent the afternoon going through them in the library."

"There's nothing in those records, is there?" he countered.

Cleo frowned. "I'm not sure how to answer that. The records contain the most complete health information we have on the patients. So there's plenty in there. But our nursing staff and care coordinators already reviewed those records and found nothing that would explain the deaths. So, no, I don't believe that

Dr. King is going to find his answer in those papers. But I'm not an expert."

The answer satisfied Roger. "Thanks. Go on."

"While I gathered the files, he spent some time in the kitchen."

Bryce gave her a questioning look. "What on earth for?"

"According to the chef, he asked questions about the menu and any dietary restrictions of the deceased. That was one of the first things we did internally, too. We checked to make sure we were not feeding people something that was killing them. We found nothing. Chef Tonga didn't seem to think that Dr. King saw anything out of the ordinary either."

"So, this guy flew in here to redo the work we've already done and is coming up with bupkis. Great use of taxpayer dollars. Glad we didn't hire him."

Cleo shot Ron a cold look. "His field investigation has barely begun. I wouldn't expect him to have an answer for us today. Beginning tomorrow, he'd like to interview residents and staff members. He's looking for any sort of commonality among the people who died. Did they all attend the same event or use the same brand of shampoo or ... I don't know. It could be anything. He plans to tease out all these disparate factors to find the one that connects them."

She reached for her glass of water and Bryce took the opportunity to steer the conversation.

"Thank you, Miss Clarkson. The reason I called this meeting is to address Dr. King's interview request. Now, of course, our residents can speak to whomever they like about whatever they like. But we need to be remember these folks are scared, and they may well lead him on a wild goose chase with outlandish theories about what's causing the deaths. And that won't benefit us or them. It'll just prolong this time of uncertainty and continue to damage our reputation. That's why—"

"They're not scared."

"Excuse me?" Bryce was equally stunned that Arthur would interrupt him and that he'd contradict him.

Arthur cleared his throat. "I mean, of course they're scared. But they're more than scared. I've had the opportunity to talk to them through the Spread the Word ministry program. And I can tell you, folks are petrified. Some of them aren't sleeping. Some of them aren't eating. Some of them—like my own grandmother—are on the verge of hysteria. It's really bad." Arthur fell silent and turned his pen in a circle on the table.

"That's not an inaccurate characterization," Cleo agreed in a soft voice.

"Well, Arthur, you're supposed to be quelling that terror through the outreach program," Bryce said pointedly.

Arthur met his eyes, gray-faced. "I'm trying. And the lay ministers working with me are giving it everything they have. But the residents don't exactly find comfort in our message that the home they live in is in the grips of Satan, pastor."

Bryce wasn't certain whether he imagined the note of rebuke in Arthur's voice or if it was real. He glanced around the table. No one else appeared to be taken aback; he decided to let it slide.

"I can understand the situation is likely causing the residents to do some soul-searching. It's your job to provide biblical answers to their questions in this time of need."

Arthur nodded, although his expression suggested he had more to say.

Bryce went on, "Getting back to the interviews. We don't want these terrified residents to worsen the situation in their hysteria. So I propose that Ms. Clarkson and I sit in on all of the interviews."

Roger frowned. "And what does our high-priced attorney have to say about that?

"Counsel hasn't weighed in yet," Cleo explained. "They have an associate researching the issue and promised to get us a memo in the morning." She straightened her shoulders and sat up very tall before continuing. "But I've shared my own reservations about doing so with Pastor Bryce. I think our guests need to feel that they can speak to Dr. King freely and in confidence."

The room fell completely silent.

After a long pause, Ron said, "Sorry, Bryce. I gotta say I'm with Miss Clarkson on this one. We don't want it to look like we're censoring or directing what folks say to this Dr. King. It makes everything look worse. Makes us look like we're trying to cover something up. Like we're guilty."

Bryce glanced around the table. Then he said, "Let's put it to a vote. I move we authorize representatives of the church and the assisted care facility to sit in on Dr. King's interviews with the residents to protect our interests and our reputation."

"Do we have a second?" Becki asked.

"Seconded," Charlene said.

"All those in favor say 'aye'."

"Aye," he began.

Charlene and Philomena chimed in together, "Aye."

Bryce waited.

Arthur dropped his eyes to the table, but Ron and Roger met his stare.

"You're both nays?"

"Afraid so, Bryce."

"Me, too, pastor."

Bryce's nostrils flared. "And you, Arthur?"

He nodded mutely.

Becki said in a low voice, "So that's three in favor and four opposed. The motion fails." She quickly returned her eyes to her iPad.

Philomena raised her hand. "Can I say something?"

"Please," Bryce told her.

"That might be all well and good for the residents. But speaking for myself, as an employee, I don't want to be interviewed without somebody there in my corner. I was on shift when those people died, you know."

Bryce flicked his gaze to Cleo, who wore a thoughtful expression.

"I suppose, that, upon request by an employee, having a representative with them would be fine. Assuming legal counsel signs off, of course."

"Of course. We pay them too much not to take their advice," Bryce intoned.

Philomena was nodding eagerly. "I'd also like you to be there if I'm interviewed. I'm afraid people aren't going to understand our outreach, especially after what happened at the beginning of the month with Mr.—"

"I understand. Unless the lawyers tell me I can't, I will personally sit in the room with each of you," Bryce promised. "Plus, I'm fairly certain you can't be compelled to talk to anybody if you really don't want to."

Beside him Cleo's eyes narrowed with just the faintest tightening of the skin right at the corners.

After a moment, she said coolly, "If no one else has any additional questions for me, I do need to leave. I have a meeting on Sugarloaf Key."

She glanced at her bracelet watch. Bryce took a moment to wonder what kind of meeting she could be having at this hour of the night then pushed the thought away. Cleo Clarkson's personal rendezvous was not his concern.

"That's really all I had. Does anyone else have any further business?" he asked, looking around the table.

Nobody spoke.

"Hearing nothing, the meeting will adjourn after a brief prayer."

Cleo stopped gathering her purse and belongings and lowered herself back into her chair.

Eight heads bowed.

"Heavenly Father, thank you for guiding us in our decisions during this meeting. We will go forth and glorify Your Name and Your Kingdom through our abundant and prosperous lives. Please bless us and shower us with riches. Amen."

CHAPTER NINETEEN

Arthur hung back as the others filed out of the room.

Cleo Clarkson swept out first, her high heels clattering hurriedly along the hallway. She was followed by Philomena and Charlene who left engaged in conversation about where to get a piece of pie and a cup of coffee at this hour. Ron and Roger stuck around to chat with Pastor Bryce about some golf outing.

Arthur shifted his weight nervously from side to side, wishing they would wrap up their conversation before he lost his nerve. Finally the three men slapped one another on the back heartily and the others left. Now it was just him, Pastor Scott, and his assistant Becki.

Becki was powering down her device and packing

up her bag. Pastor Bryce scrolled through his messages on his phone. Arthur crossed the room.

"Pastor Bryce, if you have a minute?"

The pastor looked up from his phone. "What can I do for you Arthur? Is this about your buy-in?"

Arthur glanced at Becki who was studiously avoiding his gaze, her attention focused on the table.

"No, it's not about that. But I'm going to have it soon. Very, very soon."

"Let's hope so, Arthur."

Arthur wasn't sure how to respond to that, so he forged ahead. "Sir, I just wondered if I could ask ... Well, Ms. Rivers mentioned that something happened at Golden Shores earlier this month."

"Yes?" Pastor Scott said blankly.

Arthur shoved his hands in his pocket and balled them into fists while he screwed up his courage. "Well, what did happen?"

Pastor Scott didn't answer for a moment.

Arthur could hear the fast beat of his heart and the slow tick of the clock on the wall. Sweat beaded on his forehead.

Finally, after an interminable pause, Pastor Bryce said, "I have no idea. I imagine the first death."

Then he turned to Becki. "Let's go."

Becki's eyes darted from Pastor Bryce's face to Arthur's and back again. "Yes, sir."

They headed for the door.

"Wait." Arthur winced at his own commanding tone.

Pastor Bryce turned slowly on his heel. "Yes?"

"Please, Pastor Bryce. What's going on at Golden Shores? My grandmother is there. She's beside herself with fear. I need to know if she's safe. I have to give her some comfort, some assurance—"

"What you have to do—if you truly love your grandmother and you want to help and protect her—is convince her to give you the money to buy into the ministry. God will bless her for doing so, Arthur. It's that simple."

"I'm trying. But she's scared. I need to ease her fears."

Pastor Bryce gave him a look that was a mixture of disappointment and wonder. "No, Arthur, you don't."

"Excuse me?"

"Fear is a great motivator. You know the saying, it is better to be feared than to be loved. Well, a fearful heart is a heart that will pay a price to find love. Your grandmother needs the Lord's protection. Her Catholicism can't help her. Not now, not with the evil forces that have been unleashed at Golden Shores. She needs the grace that only our church can give her. You need to convert your grandmother and she needs to invest in your ministry. Use that fear. Use it and close the deal."

Pastor Bryce strolled out of the room with Becki trailing along behind him.

Arthur stood stock still and slack-jawed. So much for his Saint Sebastian candle.

CHAPTER TWENTY

C leo hesitated in the doorway and surveyed the noisy bar. A smattering of off-season tourists sat at tables on the patio, laughing and singing along with the steel drum band. Inside, the tables were closer together and occupied by locals, most of whom nursed their drinks with necks craned back and their eyes fixed on the sports channels that played on the televisions hanging near the ceiling. For a moment, she thought she'd been stood up. Then she spotted him.

Bodhi King sat at a small table squeezed into a dim corner behind the long bar. He was reading. His head was bent over a computer printout. He held a pen in his right hand and a sweating glass in his left.

She ran her hands down her thighs in a useless effort to smooth out the linen fabric, flipped her hair over her shoulder, and marched past the row of solitary drinkers who lined the bar on stools.

One benefit of the volume level was that she couldn't quite make out the leering comments lobbed her way. She sidestepped a harried waiter balancing a heavy tray of food and came around the end of the bar.

As she reached the table, Bodhi looked up. He put down the pen and stood to greet her.

"I can't believe you can get any reading done in this place," she said as she slipped into the chair across from him.

"It's just a matter of focusing." He eased the papers into a folder and placed it inside a duffle bag that had been jammed under his chair.

"Is that your luggage?"

"Yes. I'm staying with Dr. Ashland across the street, so I figured I'd just carry it over with me."

She took in the empty beer bottles on the table then scanned the room. "Have he and Detective Williams left?"

"You just missed them."

Finally. At last, *something* had gone her way.

She'd been dreading facing Felicia Williams ever since she'd left the miserable church meeting. To say the detective didn't like her was a wild understatement.

A waitress swung by. "Can I get you something? Joel said to just add it to his tab," she said as she cleared the empty bottles from the table.

Cleo eyed Bodhi's glass. He slid a menu across the table.

"I'm having club soda, but please, get what you want. And you should take advantage of Dr. Ashland's offer—the food's pretty good."

She scanned the entrees. "It *has* been a long week —and it's only Tuesday. I'll have a gin and tonic and the fish tacos, please."

"You got it."

As the waitress walked off, Cleo rolled her shoulders to release some tension then tilted her head, first to one side then to the other, to stretch her neck.

"You're under a lot of stress," Bodhi observed quietly.

She shrugged. "Sure. I mean, wouldn't you be? I'm the director of a facility that's losing, on average, 1.25 patients a week."

"It's more than that, though. Your eyes have a haunted quality."

"I'm worried. I don't want any more of my guests to die," she stammered. "I care about them. And they're scared. It's casting a pall over the entire place."

The waitress returned with her drink. "Your tacos'll be up in a flash."

Cleo smiled and sipped the tart drink. "Thanks." She waited until the woman had left then said, "I can't stop wondering ..."

"What are you wondering?"

"What if the cause of death isn't some environmental factor or shared trait? What if ... what if someone's killing these people, deliberately?"

He studied her face. "Do you have some reason to believe there's a murderer working at Golden Shores?"

"No. I mean, I don't know. I know the police are investigating the staff—that seems to suggest there could be. Doesn't it?"

"Maybe. Not necessarily. It's Detective Williams's job to run down all the angles. Of course she's going to look at the people who work there. Is it possible there's a killer on the staff? Sure."

She picked up her glass and took a long swallow.

"But I'd say it's unlikely."

"Why?"

"There just aren't any signs of foul play. Let's say one of your nurses or aides was killing patients in a way that left no obvious, outward signs. Maybe poisoning or smothering them with a pillow."

He paused, and she nodded. Her throat was too tight, she couldn't speak at the moment.

"I'd still expect Dr. Ashland to find forensic evidence of toxicity or asphyxia."

Her morbid curiosity loosened her tongue. "Such as?"

"It's hard to establish asphyxia from smothering. I suppose that's why so many movie villains or killers in mystery novels choose it. There's no mess, no blood or visible bruising. And if the victim had a weak heart and died quickly from cardiac arrest, there might not be signs of asphyxiation because the heart would quit working first. But, assuming the actual cause of death was asphyxia, I'd expect to see cyanosis—that's the blueish discoloration of the skin. There's some disagreement in the field as to whether smothering asphyxiation would cause the petechial hemorrhages we see in strangulation or positional asphyxiation, but none of the dead had cyanosis or petechial hemorrhaging—broken blood vessels."

His matter-of-fact certainty surprised her.

"But that's not determinative, is it? The absence of a thing?" She pressed him as she dug into the tacos that had appeared on the table without her noticing during their conversation.

"Is the absence of a thing determinative? That

depends on whether I answer as a forensic pathologist or as a Buddhist." He laughed quietly then grew serious. "But, no, I wouldn't rule out smothering on that basis. I *would* rule it out because of those rictus grins ... I can't see how the facial muscles could form that mask while being compressed with a pillow. Generally, a smotherer would close the victim's lips and mouth first, anyway. Otherwise, it would take a very long time."

"Oh. Right."

The surreality of eating fish tacos at a local bar near the water while casually discussing methods of murder with a guy like Bodhi King suddenly hit her. Or maybe it was the gin. Either way, she felt woozy and warm.

"Do you need air?" he asked right away.

She shook her head and took a slow, deep breath. Then she said, "No. I'm okay. Sorry about that."

He leaned across the table and pierced her with a long look. "Don't apologize. This is a lot to take in. And it's got to be hard for you. I can tell you really care about your guests."

"I consider them to be friends. Actually, some of them are more like family to me," she said softly. Her appetite gone, she pushed the plate away.

"Cleo, I understand. I'm here to help. Tomorrow, Detective Williams will talk to the employees who were working when these people died. You, and they, shouldn't think that's because they're under suspicion. They're simply the ones who are likely to have the most information to offer. And I'd like to start talking to residents."

She snapped back to attention. "Right. I have a list. I'd suggest starting with Julia Martin, Lynette Johnson, and Hector Santiago. They were all close with the guests who died. Well, four of them, at least."

"Oh?"

"Yes, Mr. Gonzales—the first person who died—wasn't in their group."

"What sort of group?" he probed.

"They're all Catholics—I mean, we have lots of Catholic guests. Father Rafael actually comes over and says a Mass for them. But, the seven of them used to get together and do service projects like they used to when they were in the parish. They call it their social group."

"But not Mr. Gonzales?"

"Right," she confirmed.

"Hmm." He fell quiet, obviously lost in thought.

She twisted her napkin in her lap while she waited for him to look up.

It's now or never, she told herself.

"You know how I said some of my guests are like family to me?"

"Yes."

She tried to ignore the rapid flutter of her pulse. "Actually, one of them *is* family, but he doesn't know it."

Bodhi tilted his head and gave her a questioning look.

"Mr. Santiago is my biological grandfather—he's my father's father. But I was adopted as a baby. He doesn't even know he has a granddaughter." Tears filled her eyes. "Bodhi, I just found him. I can't lose him to ... whatever's happening at Golden Shores."

CHAPTER TWENTY-ONE

But the fruit of the Spirit is love, joy,
peace, forbearance, kindness,
goodness, faithfulness, gentleness,
self-control. Against such there is
no law.

GALATIANS 5:22-23

We will develop and cultivate the
liberation of mind by loving
kindness, make it our vehicle, make
it our basis, stabilize it, exercise
ourselves in it, and fully perfect it.

THE BUDDHA, SUTTA PITAKA

Bodhi sat crossed-legged on the iron bench and arranged his limbs into a comfortable position. He softened his face. He took note of the slight chill that blew across the water on the pre-dawn air. Finally, he relaxed his breathing and allowed his eyelids to close.

Once his mind was clear of thought, he began the loving kindness (*metta bhavana*) meditation.

He began by silently reciting the words that set a calm mind and a kind heart as his intention for the day. Then he turned his thoughts toward loved ones— family and friends, old and new, wishing them well in his mind.

He thought of the people he'd met in the past twenty-four hours—Detective Williams, Dr. Ashland, Cleo, Lynette, Chef Tonga, and Stacey. He extended warm wishes to them. And then to the families of Mr. Garcia, Ms. Morales, Mr. Gonzales, Mrs. Ruiz, and Mr. Caldron—the men and women who'd died at Golden Shores. He held each of them in his mind and hoped for peace for them.

Finally, he thought of the residents and employees of Golden Shores who were strangers to them. He considered the turmoil and uncertainty they might be feeling, the fear and anxiety. He shifted his focus to how those stressful feelings might be eased.

His mind returned to Felicia Williams and Cleo Clarkson and the enmity between them. He felt his brow furrow, and he smoothed it. He wished the two women could find peace and happiness and, perhaps, even make peace. Could he be a bridge between them? He set the thought aside for now.

When he felt certain he could approach everyone he met during the coming day with appropriate empathy and kindness, he opened his eyes.

The sun had just begun its journey over the water. Low, heavy clouds created bands of pink and orange light that hung over the glistening water. He heard the slap of flip-flops against skin and turned to see Joel Ashland crossing the beach with a mug in each hand. Steam rose from his hot beverages in wisps that vanished into the chilly air.

"I thought I might find you down here," Dr. Ashland said in a low voice, as though he didn't want to wake any nearby birds or fish.

"There's something about seeing the sun come up over the water that seems to help a person start the day in the right frame of mind," Bodhi said.

"Yes, there is. It's my routine to come down here with my morning coffee and get myself set for the day ahead." He thrust one of the mugs toward Bodhi. "Here you go. I didn't imagine you'd be a coffee drinker. But I had some good tea from India in the kitchen. I made you a mug."

"Thank you."

Bodhi cupped his hands around the mug and let its heat radiate through him. He sniffed the steam rising from the liquid and caught a hint of spice that woke his senses. He sipped the beverage and gave a small sigh of pleasure.

"Told you it was the good stuff. I was dating a woman for a while who brought it back from Agra. The romance didn't last, but I'm still finding her things all over the camper." Dr. Ashland laughed ruefully.

They sat in comfortable silence for several moments drinking their hot drinks and watching the sun fully rise and its rays paint the water with light.

After a few minutes, Dr. Ashland spoke again. "I was asleep when you got in last night from your hot date."

Bodhi opened his mouth to correct the medical examiner. Then he noticed the twinkle in Dr. Ashland's eyes and said nothing.

Dr. Ashland went on. "But while you were living it up at Mangrove Mama's, some of us were working. I logged into my case files remotely and took a close look at the photographs I took of each of the deceased."

Bodhi's mind returned to the autopsy of Carlos Garcia the previous afternoon. He remembered that Dr. Ashland had taken several photographs extreme close-up photographs of Mr. Garcia's face in an effort to memorialize the rictus grin.

"Did you find anything interesting?"

Any hint of joking disappeared from Dr. Ashland's demeanor. "No, I didn't. And I paid particular attention to their eyes."

"No Kayser-Fleischer ring?"

"Not a one."

Bodhi felt a ripple of disappointment travel through him. He hadn't been wedded to Wilson disease as an explanation for the death cluster, but it had been the most likely explanation he'd come across thus far.

"Well, I guess ruling something out conclusively is almost as much progress as ruling something in."

Dr. Ashland snorted. "You might be able to convince a layperson that you believe that. But we both know if we'd have been able to point to copper overload, our work would be done, and those people at Golden Shores would be able to breathe easy again."

"True," Bodhi admitted.

He turned his attention to the water and allowed himself to get lost in the gentle tug of the waves against the rocks at the edge of the shore.

"I can't justify going forward with genetic testing to see if there's a mutation without some physical evidence to back it up," Dr. Ashland explained.

"Of course not. It wouldn't be a responsible use of your resources."

They both knew sequencing the ATP7B gene from potentially degraded, postmortem samples would be expensive and time-consuming.

"But there's still a chance."

Bodhi turned his attention away from the water and back to the man sitting beside him. "A chance it's Wilson disease?"

"Right. Maybe the dark brown pigmentation of their eye color, which they all share, masked the ring. Or maybe this is lightning in a bottle, and we have a cluster of people who died of Wilson disease without showing signs of liver failure or evidence of copper deposits in their eyes or organs."

Bodhi gave him a close look. "That would be so statistically unlikely as to be nearly impossible."

"Yup." Dr. Ashland nodded his agreement. "But nearly impossible and impossible aren't the same thing. Could be a black swan event."

Bodhi considered this theory. A 'black swan' was a term initially coined by economists to describe an unexpected event that wasn't thought possible until after it happened. Five unrelated, elderly people dying of Wilson disease in a month's time without exhibiting its primary symptoms would certainly qualify.

"Well," he said slowly, "today I'll be interviewing some residents who were close with the deceased. I'll ask whether any of the dead exhibited any neurological or psychological changes in the period before they died. Would information of that sort tilt the budgetary considerations?"

A smile broke across Dr. Ashland's face, and he slapped Bodhi's back so heartily that coffee sloshed over the side of his mug.

"If you get confirmation of any behavioral changes, I'll have something to hang my hat on to stretch my budget to do the sequencing. In the meantime, I'll make sure I keep good frozen specimens in case we need them."

A calm settled over Bodhi as they agreed on their plan. He stood and took one last look at the water to sear its tranquil beauty into his memory.

They turned and began to wend their way up the narrow beach to the short gravel path that led to the silver camper.

As they reached the path, Detective Williams's dark sedan careened down from the highway and turned into the campground.

"Here comes your ride," Dr. Ashland remarked as the car stopped at the guard booth at the entrance.

Bodhi gave him a sidelong look. "Do you mind if I ask you something?"

"Suppose it depends on what you ask."

"It's not case related, but I'm trying to understand something. I thought you might be able to shed some light for an out-of-towner."

"I'll give it a shot."

"Is there some history between Detective Williams and Cleo Clarkson I should know about? I get the impression that they don't care much for one another."

Dr. Ashland roared with laughter. "Oh, is that the impression you get? Because the impression I get is that those two women would like nothing more than to run into each other in a dark alley with no witnesses."

Bodhi half-smiled. "I may have understated the situation. But what gives?"

Dr. Ashland blew out a breath and kept his eyes on Detective Williams's approaching car while he answered. "Felicia doesn't exactly confide in me. But if I had to guess I'd say she doesn't appreciate Cleo's, shall we say, natural attributes."

"You're saying Detective Williams is jealous of Cleo because of the way she looks? She doesn't strike me as shallow or petty."

"No, that's true. Felicia is about as deep as they come. But she is still a human being. And somebody like Cleo Clarkson, well, people respond to her in a different way than they respond to Felicia."

Bodhi thought about Cleo's exuberant warmth and Detective Williams off-putting frostiness. "Couldn't that be a function of personality more than one of appearance?"

"Which came first—the chicken or the egg? I'm obviously not an expert on the fairer sex. Miss Indian Tea's parting words to me were that I was an over-grown man-child stuck in the seventies. And Felicia doesn't seem to like me very much. So, what do I know? But other than human nature being what it is, as far as I know there's no other reason for the enmity between them."

They reached the front door of the camper just as Detective Williams pulled up alongside it.

"I just have to run in and get my bag," Bodhi said. "Will you let Detective Williams know I'll be right out? And thanks for the tea."

He raised the empty mug in a salute and stepped up to the door.

"You're more than welcome. And here's a piece of free advice as a chaser. If I were you, I wouldn't spend a whole lot of time trying to figure out why there's bad blood between Cleo and Felicia. Just make sure you don't get between them and end up as collateral damage."

Bodhi nodded his understanding and went inside. The medical examiner turned to greet Detective Williams.

CHAPTER TWENTY-TWO

Either Bodhi's little meeting with Cleo Clarkson hadn't gone very well, or return visitors to Golden Shores didn't merit the royal treatment. After taking the public ferry—no yacht—from Big Pine, Felicia and Bodhi docked at Golden Island and were greeted by ... no one. Unless you counted the gulls.

"Where's your girlfriend?"

Bodhi wrinkled his forehead but didn't respond. He stepped off the boat, slung the strap of his laptop bag over his shoulder, then held out a hand to help her off the ferry.

A hot pulse of embarrassment surged through her at her pettiness. She ducked her head and ignored his hand.

They started to walk up the path to the building.

The autumn air was just as humid and gross as the winter, spring, and summer air. She wondered idly what it would be like to live where the seasons truly changed.

"I suspect Cleo's busy setting up our meetings," Bodhi suddenly said.

"What?" She turned her head.

"You asked where my girlfriend was. I assume you meant Cleo. I'm guessing she's got her hands full lining up the people we asked to speak to."

"Oh. Right." Now she felt stupid on top of everything else. "I was just joking."

"Mmm."

They walked in silence. It occurred to Felicia that she needed a reset for the day. She could feel herself spiraling into nastiness. She peeked at Bodhi. He was taking in the flowers and birds as they walked, paying almost no mind to her.

What the heck? It couldn't hurt.

She slowed her step, closed her eyes, and found her breath. As she inhaled, she thought 'calm.' As she exhaled, she thought 'steady.' She repeated the in breath, out breath sequence, feeling her crankiness slide away.

She stumbled over a loose shell. A strong hand

gripped her elbow and steadied her. She opened her eyes.

Bodhi was smiling at her. "Walking meditation—it's a great tool. Pro tip: most people do it with their eyes open."

Laughter welled up inside her then burst forward, like a fountain. Amid her waves of laughter, she gasped "Right ... I'll remember that."

"You have the most melodic laugh I've ever heard. It sounds like music."

They reached the lobby doors. She gaped at him for a moment then mumbled, "Thanks."

She hurriedly pressed the buzzer to announce their arrival.

The cheerful man behind the visitor's desk greeted them by name and handed them each a temporary ID badge. "Miss Clarkson thought it would be easier if you could access the entire building without an escort or calling ahead. So you are now free to roam about. She did say to send you to her office when you get here, though. Do you know where you're going?"

"We do. Thank you," Bodhi said.

They affixed their badges to their shirts then followed the quiet hallway behind the desk to Cleo's office.

Her door was ajar. She sat at her desk with a stack of documents in front of her.

"Good morning," Bodhi said.

Cleo looked up. Felicia could see faint blue smudges under her brilliant green eyes.

"Bodhi, Detective Williams. Can I offer you a coffee or a glass of water?"

"No, thank you."

"I'm fine."

Cleo stood and smiled. "I'm sure you're itching to get started. I asked Mrs. Pearl and Mrs. Rivers to come in this morning to talk to Detective Williams. They're already here."

"Great. Lead the way," Felicia said briskly.

"Nurse Martinez is on his way in, as well," Cleo added.

Felicia's stomach clenched, but she just nodded and maintained her focus on the tasks ahead. "I'd also like to speak to Pastor Scott, if you can arrange that."

Cleo raised her eyebrows. "It must be your lucky day. I was just about to tell you that he's decided to sit in on your interviews with Philomena and Charlene."

"That's not necessary. Nor is it desirable," Felicia said with all the diplomacy she could muster, which, admittedly, wasn't much.

Some emotion flickered in Cleo's eyes. Distress?

Felicia couldn't be sure because it vanished as quickly as it had appeared.

"I'm afraid it's a condition of the interview. Our legal counsel has said they are entitled to have a company representative with them if they like, and both Philomena and Charlene have requested Pastor Scott."

Felicia frowned. "I'm not sure your attorneys are right on this one."

But Bodhi had a different concern. "Is Pastor Scott a representative of the company? I didn't realize he took an active role in your operations?"

Cleo's expression was pained. "It's ... complicated. I realize the situation may be unconventional. And the police department can always go to a judge and get an order, I suppose. But if you want the interviews to go forward today, Pastor Scott will be in the room. And Philomena and Charlene are already here ..."

Felicia sighed. Cleo was right, and they both knew it. She could go ahead with the interviews and deal with Pastor Scott or she could waste a week trying to get them on her own terms.

"Fine. But I plan to ask him some questions, too."

Cleo shrugged. Then she turned to Bodhi. "Mrs. Martin, Mrs. Johnson, and Mr. Santiago know you'd like to chat with them. They're at the cafe having breakfast right now, but they said they're free all morning. Actually, they were planning to meet anyway. Their social club is getting ready for a community service project with some teenagers in Key Largo. So they've already got a room reserved in the library. You can meet with them one at a time or all together."

Bodhi smiled. "Handy."

"Sometimes things just work out. Let me show Detective Williams to the conference room and then I'll take you down to—"

Lynette poked her head into the room. "Was it delivered?" She looked around. "Oh, sorry to interrupt. Good morning, Dr. King."

"Lynette, this is Detective Williams," Cleo said as she reached for an insulated bag that sat on the credenza behind her desk. "Here you go. Could you take Dr. King down to the cafe with you? That way he won't have to cool his heels while I get Detective Williams set up."

Lynette took the cooler bag in both hands. "Sure. Follow me, Doc."

Bodhi caught Felicia's eye on his way out. "Good luck."

"Back at you," she said. Maybe today would be the day her investigation finally caught a break.

"So what's in the bag?" Bodhi asked when Lynette paused for a breath in her tour guide spiel.

She patted the silver bag at her side. "My breakfast. I think today's special was an acacia, oat, and berry bowl. Lunch and dinner are in here, too. Chef Tonga will stow those in the refrigerator for me."

"You order in—from one of the Keys?"

"I do now. Nothing against the chef, but folks are dropping like flies. I'm not eating or drinking anything that's not sealed until you figure out what's going on." She gave him a meaningful look.

He couldn't fault her logic. Even though there was no evidence that anyone had been poisoned by or fallen ill from the food, it was a reasonable precaution.

"Plus, it's better for me. Not so fatty. Don't tell the chef," she whispered with a laugh.

He got the feeling she was making light of her ordered-in meals to avoid coming across as paranoid. He suspected her anxiety level was higher than she let on.

They entered the cafe, which looked more like an upscale restaurant than an institutional cafeteria. Instead of long, communal tables, two tops, four tops, and the occasional longer rectangle were scattered throughout the room. The morning light streamed through the large windows.

Lynette led him to a square table for four in the front left corner of the room. The man and woman already seated at the table waved as they approached.

"Morning, Lyn," the man boomed.

"Hector, Julia," she replied. "This is Dr. King."

Hector used the table for leverage and pushed himself to standing.

"Dr. King, it's a pleasure."

Bodhi shook the man's outstretched hand. "The pleasure's mine, Mr. Santiago."

He searched the man's wrinkled face for a hint of resemblance to his granddaughter but saw none—except perhaps for his warm manner.

"And you must be Mrs. Martin," Bodhi said, turning to the seated woman to Mr. Santiago's left.

She smiled. "It's nice to meet you. We're all so relieved you're here." Her voice quavered.

"Let me just drop off my food with Chef Tonga then we can chat." Lynette placed her breakfast bowl on the table then started to turn toward the big double doors that led to the kitchen.

Bodhi intercepted her and gestured toward the

bag. "Why don't I do that for you? You sit down and eat. I have a question for the chef anyway."

She lobbed the bag in his direction and plopped into a chair. "Don't have to ask me twice. Thanks."

He deposited his laptop bag on the seat of the free chair and headed for the kitchen with Lynette's meals.

He pushed the doors open. They swung freely. Two prep chefs—one male, one female—raised their heads from their cutting boards.

"Is Chef Tonga around?"

The female chef jabbed the thumb of her free hand over her shoulder without stopping the chopping motion of her knife hand.

"He's in the pantry—back there."

Bodhi crossed the gleaming kitchen and entered a cavernous space. The walls were covered with floor-to-ceiling wire shelving. The shelves were crammed with spices, dry goods, canned goods, oils, bins of root vegetables, and every imaginable staple.

Pedro Tonga was pawing through a bin of what appeared to be beets, muttering under his breath.

"Excuse me, chef."

He turned. "Ah, Dr. King." He dumped a handful of beets into a basket. "Did you need something?"

"Two things, actually. First, I have Mrs. Johnson's

meals. She said they could go in your refrigerator?" He raised the bag and gave the chef a questioning look.

"Bah, her organic superfoods." He made a face and waved a dismissive hand toward the two refrigerators around the corner in the main kitchen.

Bodhi walked back to the refrigerators, opened the closest door, and placed the insulated bag on a shelf next to a large roast resting in a copper pan.

"And the second thing?" the chef said from just behind Bodhi's shoulder, his voice matching his stride for quickness. He was a man in a perpetual hurry.

"The second thing is a favor."

Chef Tonga pursed his lips. "What sort of favor?"

"Could you, just temporarily, switch from using copper pots, pans, utensils, and serving trays? Just until I confirm a theory. Do you have any cast iron hidden away anywhere?"

Bodhi was sure he did. The chef had no doubt had to buy the mass of shiny copperware in bulk to replace his trusty workhorses.

Something like excitement glinted in Pedro Tonga's eyes. "Pastor Scott approved this?"

Bodhi shook his head somberly. "Pastor Scott doesn't know." He paused then added, "But it's important. And sometimes, chef, it's better to ask forgiveness than permission."

"Forgiveness instead of permission, eh?" he mused.

After a moment, he snapped his fingers and shouted to the prep chefs. "Go into the storage and bring out my Le Creuset."

The male chef bobbed his head. "Which pieces, chef?"

"All of it." Chef Tonga smiled.

CHAPTER TWENTY-THREE

Bodhi rejoined the group huddled around the table. Lynette was halfway through her breakfast, and someone had already cleared away the dishes that had been in front of Mrs. Martin and Mr. Santiago. They each sipped a cup of coffee.

"Lynette's about finished. When she's done, we'll go over to the library where we can talk in private," Mr. Santiago informed him.

"We reserved a room for our social club," Mrs. Martin added.

"Great." He moved his computer bag aside and took his seat. "Don't hurry, Lynette. Enjoy your meal. Maybe someone can fill me in on your social club in the meantime? Just give me some basic background."

"Sure. Julia, you're the secretary. You want to do it?" Mr. Santiago asked deferentially.

"Okay. We all went to the same church before we moved in here—Saint Lazarus's Shrine in Key West. We were part of a study group there under Father Rafael. Now, we're more of a book club or a social club. We pray together, and we sometimes organize a service project or support a charity. The first Sunday of the month, after Father Rafael's weekly service here, we get together with him."

Mrs. Martin explained confidently, but Bodhi caught her sneaking a peek at Lynette, as if for approval.

"And the others—the deceased, they were also all Catholic?" he asked.

"No. Not José," Mr. Santiago quickly corrected him.

"Right. José Gonzales," Bodhi amended. "Was he a member of the Golden Island Church, then?"

Lynette did a spit take, shooting a spray of mineral water onto the tablecloth.

"Sorry," she choked. "No. José was most definitely *not* a member of Golden Island."

Mr. Santiago shook his head at her reaction. Bodhi make a mental note to follow up on Mr. Gonzales's beliefs then turned back to Mrs. Martin.

"But Mr. Garcia, Ms. Morales, Mrs. Ruiz, and Mr. Caldron were all Roman Catholics, right?"

"Yes," she confirmed.

"And had they all been parishioners at Saint Sebastian's?"

"Yes. Well, Ms. Morales was more of a Christmas and Easter Catholic than a regular churchgoer—until she and Carlos got together," Mrs. Martin elaborated.

"And were they all members of your study group back then?"

"Again, everyone except Esmerelda. She started dating Carlos when she moved in here. And he started bringing her along to our little meetings. Most of us didn't mind," Lynette said, giving Julia Martin a side-eye.

"She didn't care about religion. She just wanted someone to warm her bed," Mrs. Martin retorted.

Mr. Santiago cleared his throat. "If you're done eating, Lyn, we should move this party to the library."

Lynette pushed her bowl away and picked up her water bottle. "Let's go. We need to do this before Hector's nap time."

Mrs. Martin tittered.

"I just need to rest for twenty minutes before lunch. You'd think I asked for a nap mat and a back rub, for crying out loud."

"He's not sleeping," Mrs. Martin confided to Bodhi as their little group wound through the tables to the exit. "He stays up all night so nothing—or nobody—can kill him in his sleep."

———

As soon as they entered the private room tucked into the far end of the library, Lynette closed the door and locked it. The atmosphere instantly crackled with secrecy and excitement.

Bodhi observed quietly as Hector Santiago drew the blinds across the large rectangular window that overlooked a garden with a water feature. Mrs. Martin opened a set of cabinets along the wall near the door and took out an MP3 player and a portable speaker. She set them up, and mambo music filled the air.

"We usually play religious music, but we've found the horns cover voices well. In case anyone's eaves-dropping," Lynette told him.

Bodhi lowered himself into a chair. He knew he wore a bemused expression, but it seemed appropriate.

"So ... what kind of social club is this, exactly?" he asked.

Lynette cackled. Soon Mr. Santiago and Mrs. Martin joined in.

When their laughter died down, Lynette looked

him squarely in the eye and said, "Here's the deal. We need your help. So we're going to let you in on a little secret. But it's not for public consumption."

He considered this. "I may have to tell Detective Williams—and possibly Dr. Ashland."

Lynette nodded. "We figured as much. We'd just ask that they keep it confidential unless and until it becomes material to a homicide investigation."

Mr. Santiago chuckled. "There she goes being all lawyerly."

"That's fair. What about Ms. Clarkson? Can I share what you tell me with her?"

A look traveled among the three residents.

Mr. Santiago shook his head. "Now don't get the wrong impression, we like Cleo. She's a good kid. A great kid. But in this instance, she's working for The Man. The Establishment."

"She really is a lovely person," Mrs. Martin added.

"And it's not that we don't trust her. We just can't put her in the situation this knowledge would put her in. It wouldn't be fair," Lynette explained.

Bodhi had always thought he had no interest in gossip, secrets, or clandestine affairs. But he would have agreed to just about any terms to find out what these three were keeping under wraps in an unassuming library meeting room.

"Okay. I won't tell her anything."

"Good. We are a little Roman Catholic social club," Lynette said.

"Okay."

"But we're also practitioners of Santería."

Bodhi didn't know what he'd been expecting, but it wasn't that.

"You are?"

"Yes. And so were Carlos, Esmerelda, and Juan Caldron, and Lucinda Ruiz."

All of the dead had practiced Santería.

"But not Mr. Gonzales," he said.

"Not Mr. Gonzales," Mr. Santiago confirmed.

"There are other Catholics living here," Lynette told him. "Quite a few."

"But as far as we know, we're the only *aborishas*," Mrs. Martin said.

Bodhi shook his head. "I'm sorry, I'm not familiar with the term."

"No reason you would be," Mr. Santiago told him. "An *aborisha* is a practitioner who has undergone some level of initiation, but is not a full priest or priestess—a *santero* or *santera*."

"Do you have a *santero* or *santera*?"

"Not really. Not anymore. We only see him once a month in that capacity," Lynette answered.

Bodhi blinked. "Father Rafael?"

"That part can't be made public. It would be a scandal. But yes, Father Rafael came to the Saint Lazarus's Shrine from a special church in Havana—the Church of Our Lady of Regla, the Black Madonna—it's both a Catholic church *and* a Santería shrine."

"Really?"

"Yes. It's different there. The Church of the Black Madonna is *very* open about the two living side by side, unusually so. But the Catholic priests throughout the country mainly accept it as part of the culture. Santería is an officially recognized religion there, you know," Mr. Santiago explained.

"Syncretism," Bodhi said, thinking aloud.

"Exactly." Lynette beamed at him as if he were her star witness.

"And this is top secret to protect Father Rafael?"

"Him, and us. Imagine if Pastor Scott found out." Mrs. Martin shivered.

"So, how does Mr. Gonzales figure into this? Did he find out about you?" Bodhi was trying to piece it all together.

"He knew about us, of course. He was a *palero*," Lynette said.

Mrs. Martin muttered darkly.

Before Bodhi could ask for a definition of *palero,* there was a quick rap on the door.

Mrs. Martin's eyes widened and she fumbled with the music player. Mr. Santiago opened the blinds just as Lynette flung the door wide to reveal a smiling Cleo Clarkson.

"I just thought I'd stop by and see how it's going," Cleo said in her low purr of a voice.

The three residents all stared at Bodhi. He cleared his throat.

"I was about to ask whether any of these folks had noticed any changes in Mr. Gonzales's behavior or mental state," Bodhi said.

It was technically true. He *had* been about to ask before the super-secret Santería news.

A look crossed Cleo's face.

"What?" he said.

"I'll let the guests answer first," she said. She closed the door and took a seat next to Lynette.

"It's hard to say. José's mental state fluctuated between miserable and downright nasty," Mr. Santiago began.

"Mr. Santiago—" Cleo protested.

"It's true, and you know it. He wasn't a very nice man," Mrs. Martin said, fumbling with the beads around her neck. "He was a bad person."

"Now, really. It's not kind to speak ill of the dead, Mrs. Martin," Cleo gently chided her.

She faced Bodhi. "He was a bit of a curmudgeon. He got very angry if the staff moved his belongings when they cleaned. Toward the end, he became a bit of a packrat. Maybe a hoarder would be a better description."

What sorts of things did he save?" Bodhi asked.

Cleo wrinkled her nose. "All sorts of disgusting things. His belongings are still in storage. His family hasn't been out to pick them up."

Bodhi was trying to concentrate on what she was saying but the bug-eyed face that Lynette was making was distracting him. He glanced at her and she began nodding urgently and pointing toward herself and then toward him. She very clearly had something to tell him about Mr. Gonzales. Something she didn't want to say in front of Cleo.

Cleo stood suddenly. "The storage closet is just around the corner. Why don't I show you? Then I'll take you upstairs to meet Detective Williams."

"I'm not quite finished here," he said.

Her face clouded. "Oh. Could you come back in a bit then? I need to meet Nurse Martinez when he arrives. He's about to get on the ferry now. That ought to be enough time to show you Mr. Gonzales's ...

collection. Then you could finish up with these fine folks."

"That would be fine," Mrs. Martin said.

"Are you sure?" Cleo asked, taking a closer look at Hector Santiago. "Some of you are looking tired."

Mr. Santiago peered back into her face. "We're not the only ones, dear."

Bodhi met Lynette's eyes. "Will that work for you?"

"Sure thing," she chirped.

"Okay. After you," he told Cleo.

CHAPTER TWENTY-FOUR

Felicia smiled tightly at Charlene Rivers. "I think that's all I have for now, Mrs. Rivers. The department appreciates your coming in to talk. Before we wrap this up, do you have any final thoughts that might be helpful? Anything I neglected to ask about that you think may be relevant?"

She asked the follow-up question purely out of habit. To say the interview with Charlene Rivers had been a bust would be a charitable description.

For one thing, the woman seemed to be wholly unobservant. She didn't remember anything unusual ever happening on one of her shifts.

For another, she kept bringing all of Felicia's questions back to her church. In answer to a question about whether Mr. Garcia got a lot of visitors, she'd rambled on about the Golden Island Church's shut-in visitation program on Key Largo.

But the most irritating thing about the wasted hour and a half was Bryce Scott's incessant interruptions and coaching. If Felicia had even an inkling that the Rivers woman might know something useful, she'd have slapped a pair of shiny metal bracelets around the pastor's wrists at the outset. He was interfering with a witness interview—and was being freaking annoying about it, too.

As if on cue, he fake-coughed.

"Oh, yes, right. I did want to say one more thing," Charlene blurted.

Felicia resisted the urge to poke herself in the eye with her pen and put herself out of her misery.

"Go right ahead."

The woman's eyes darted toward Pastor Scott, who nodded. Felicia's nostrils flared, but she held her tongue.

"Well, you didn't ask if anybody else was acting suspicious."

Felicia cocked her head. "Was anyone else acting suspicious?"

"Um ... yes." Charlene stumbled over her words, paused for a moment, then picked up speed and finished her sentence in a rush. "Nurse Eduardo

Martinez requested extra shifts on two of the nights people died. That's why he was there during all the deaths. Doesn't that seem shady to you? Also, a man nurse? That's ... unusual right there. But he definitely has the strength to hold someone down and suffocate them. Most of the female nurses couldn't do that, I don't think."

She finished and shot another look at her pastor, who rewarded her with a faint smile.

Felicia's blood pressure zoomed up. She felt like a cartoon character whose neck and face were gradually getting redder and redder. She waited for the steam to shoot out of the top of her head with a train whistle sound effect.

She stood up. "We're done here. Before I thank you for your time, Mrs. Rivers, let me just say that as a female homicide detective, I don't think there's anything inherently suspicious about a person choosing a career that's been gender-stereotyped."

Charlene Rivers flinched.

She went on, "And, having seen Nurse Mumma lift a two-hundred-pound man to change his sheets, I am pretty sure even the most feminine nurse has more upper body strength than you might think."

"I was ... I'm just trying ... I wanted to be helpful," Charlene stammered.

"And you were, Mrs. Rivers," Pastor Scott assured her. "God will bless you richly for your honesty and assistance."

Charlene simpered.

Felicia walked her to the door and opened it. She stuck her head out and said, "Mrs. Pearl, we'll be with you in a moment. I need to have a word with Pastor Scott first."

Philomena Pearl looked up from her novel and blinked. Charlene scooted past Felicia and left the room at a near-jog. Felicia closed the door and tried hard to get a handle on her emotions before she turned around to rip into the richest, most connected religious leader in the Southeast.

Bodhi stood in the cramped, stuffy closet and took in its contents in a state of bewilderment. He pulled out a pen and notepad to inventory the items and record his impressions.

"*These* are Mr. Gonzales's personal effects?"

"Yes. It's really strange, isn't it?" Cleo said in a low, bemused voice.

Strange was one word for the jumble of items.

He peered into a large iron cauldron filled with

dirt. Sticks, feathers, and coins were piled inside. Beside it, a smaller cauldron held more dirt, a bead necklace, and two coconut shells. He eased the lid off a nearby box with the tip of his pen. More dirt. Metal spikes. Another strand of beads.

He lifted out a convex disk and held it up to the light for a better look.

"Is that a ...?" Cleo began, standing on her tiptoes behind him.

"I think it's a turtle shell." He returned it to the box. "There are some dolls in here, too." Several small, crude figures that appeared to be fashioned out of wooden clothespins and bits of cloth were piled together in one corner.

"It gets weirder," Cleo told him.

She pointed to a stack of boxes along the wall. "There's loads more dirt, some ceremonial-looking swords, pieces of metal and glass, and lots of beads, feathers, stones, bits of fur, globs of wax ... it's just trash."

He eyed the boxes. "Has someone gone through all of this stuff and catalogued it?"

"No. I took a quick peek at a handful of the boxes, but I didn't have time to look at all of them. We've been sort of scrambling around here this month. I figure I can have someone do it when things quiet down. Or, even better, maybe one of his relatives can come and just take it away. I could use this closet back."

"It's quite a collection."

"Is it evidence that he was mentally decompensating? I mean, who saves all this stuff?"

She had a point.

"It doesn't seem like the behavior of a well-organized mind. I'd like to talk to Nurse Martinez about Mr. Gonzales for a few minutes, since he's coming in anyway. I'll need to do a more detailed interview later, but I should finish up with the residents first."

"Of course."

"I'm going to want to photograph everything in this room. And possibly gather some samples for testing."

She gave him a puzzled look. "Sure. But, the death cluster can't be caused by boxes of dirt. I mean, can it? I'm confident nobody else was hoarding dirt and junk."

He wasn't sure what the assemblage of strange items meant. But he was sure it meant *something*.

He answered her question with one of his own. "I would imagine dirt collecting isn't a common pursuit. But do you have the belongings of any of the other deceased individuals in storage?"

"Ms. Morales's."

"I'll want to see those, too."

"I can arrange that. Are you done in here for now? Because we really should go wait for Nurse Martinez if you want to talk to him first."

He took one last look at the odd menagerie. Although it seemed to lack any rhyme or reason, there was a pattern in all this stuff. He just had to find it.

"For now."

She opened the door and stepped out into the hallway. He turned out the light and followed.

A breathless young woman in hospital scrubs was running toward them. She skidded to a stop.

"Ms. Clarkson, you need to go upstairs. That detective is *screaming* at Pastor Scott. She just threatened to arrest him."

Cleo gave Bodhi a wide-eyed look of horror. "Great."

"I'll come with you."

They took off down the hall behind the aide.

CHAPTER TWENTY-FIVE

Bryce turned to see Cleo and a lanky, curly-haired man rushing into the conference room.

"Oh, thank goodness." He was surprised by the extent of his relief, but he wasn't too proud to admit that he needed to be rescued from the fire-breathing detective.

"Pastor Scott, Detective Williams, what's going on?" Cleo asked.

"Well, Cleo, it seems the detective takes issue with my—"

Detective Williams spoke right over him. "The good pastor here is engaged in witness coaching—no, witness *tampering*—in his efforts to railroad Eduardo Martinez."

Bryce eyed her cautiously. She was still shaking with fury.

"I did no such thing. Clearly, there's been some sort of misunderstanding by the—"

"You might as well have put your hand up her butt and used her as a puppet!" Detective Williams shouted.

She pointed an accusatory finger at Philomena Pearl, who sat hunched over in her seat as if willing herself to disappear. The aide was holding back tears.

"Detective Williams, a word?" the man said in a cool voice, as if the detective were perfectly rational and not a red-faced, spittle-producing, shrieking maniac.

"I take it you're Dr. King?" Bryce asked.

The man nodded but kept his focus on Detective Williams. She let out a great whoosh of breath then followed him to the door.

She paused on the threshold to turn back and glare at Bryce. "This isn't over," she warned.

As soon as they'd left, Cleo closed the door softly behind them. Then she turned to face him.

"Pastor Scott, what happened?"

He spread his arms wide and lifted his palms toward the ceiling. "I'm sure the detective's under a great deal of pressure to get to the bottom of these unfortunate deaths, but her outburst was completely unacceptable. In fact, as a citizen, I very well may file a complaint with the police department."

He leaned into his outrage, expecting some measure of sympathy, but Cleo didn't react.

Instead, she turned away from him and crouched beside Philomena's chair. "Can you tell me what happened, Mrs. Pearl?" she asked in a gentle voice.

Philomena took a shuddering breath. "I'll try, Ms. Clarkson. The detective was already angry with Pastor Bryce when I came. After Charlene's interview, she said she needed to speak to him privately before I came in."

Philomena paused and dabbed the corners of her eyes with the tissue she'd been twisting between her hands.

She exhaled then continued, "Now, I don't know what they talked about, but Charlene told me Detective Williams got really hot at the end of her interview when she explained about Nurse Martinez."

Cleo tilted her head. "Do you know what she meant by that? What did Mrs. Rivers explain about him?"

Philomena shot Bryce a worried look. "Um ..."

"Cleo, I encouraged Charlene to be completely open and honest with the detective. Apparently, she's been harboring concerns about Eduardo Martinez," he explained.

"What types of concerns?" She directed the question to Philomena.

"I'm not sure, to be honest. But I know Pastor Bryce spoke to both of us about the fact that, aside from Charlene and me, he was the only person who was working all five times someone died. It seemed like the police might be trying to put the blame on one of the three of us. And, well, Char and I both know we didn't do anything wrong. So ..."

"So Pastor Scott told you to speculate that Nurse Martinez did?" Cleo suggested.

"That's unfair," he protested. "I shared with them a fact I learned from Nurse Mumma. That he was originally not scheduled to work two of those nights, but he requested extra hours. That seemed like pertinent information."

Cleo stood and placed a reassuring hand on Philomena's shoulder. She fixed her emerald eyes on his face.

"If you thought it was worth sharing with the authorities, surely you could have talked to Detective Williams. Don't you see how this looks? Feeding answers to witnesses? This is exactly the impression I wanted to avoid." Her voice was laced with recrimination.

He stiffened his shoulders. "I did nothing inappropriate."

One eyebrow danced up to her hairline. "What did Detective Williams say to you between the interviews?" she asked in an innocent tone.

He clamped his lips together like a child who was being reprimanded and refused to answer.

———

Felicia whirled around, knocking Bodhi's hand off her elbow. "I warned him, Bodhi. I freaking told him after the Rivers interview not to interfere and not to coach the witnesses. I *told* him I'd throw his ass in jail if he did it again. *And he did it again.*"

She was spiraling out of control, and she knew it. But her red-hot anger was driving her to lash out.

"Detective," he said in a low voice.

She didn't answer or raise her eyes from the floor.

"Felicia—"

His use of her first name startled her. She looked up.

"Listen, I'm not in the mood to focus on my breath or acknowledge my anger, okay?"

"I think your anger's not really in question. No need to note it," he said with a smile. "But tell me this, what do you think Pastor Scott's goal in coaching those women might be?"

"I already told you, he's trying to throw Ed under the bus."

"He may be. Or he may simply be trying to protect Mrs. Pearl and Mrs. Rivers. They're his congregants, right? He may feel responsible for them."

"So what? Whether his goal is to shield them or screw Ed, the end result's the same," she growled. "And Ed *is* screwed now. I can't interview him without leaning hard on him. Not after the picture they painted."

"Okay. What's your goal?"

His incessant reasonable tone was really starting to piss her off.

"What do you mean, what's my goal? To stop these people from framing Ed."

He blinked at her. Then he said slowly, "Or you could choose to make protecting Eduardo Martinez your goal."

"What difference does it make, Bodhi? Stop them

or protect him—they're the same thing." She hissed the words through clenched teeth.

"But, they're not. You're gravitating to a somewhat violent or confrontational response—to punish Pastor Scott and those two women for their efforts. That's not your only choice."

"Well, I can't do nothing. I have to do something about it."

"You could do something by doing nothing."

She huffed out a breath. "Bodhi, so help me, if you don't drop the magical, mystical bullcrap and just say what you mean, I'm going to lose it for real."

"Do nothing. Don't interview Eduardo when he gets here. Tell Cleo something more urgent came up and you'll need to reschedule."

She was stunned into silence. It seemed entirely too easy. But, she realized, postponing the interview solved her primary problem without any danger of her throttling that smarmy preacher and being brought up on police brutality charges.

"That'll work," she said in amazement.

"And, as a bonus, it happens to be true."

"Wait. What?"

"Something more urgent *has* come up. I need you to go to the medical examiner's office and bring back Dr. Ashland and a whole bunch of equipment. More than he could transport alone on the ferry. I'll write out a list."

She felt the rage that had consumed her ease its grip. "Sure thing. You write out your list. I'm going to sweet talk Cleo into lending me the yacht."

"Detective—" he warned.

She laughed lightly. "Don't worry, I said 'sweet talk,' not 'beat.'"

CHAPTER TWENTY-SIX

Bodhi stepped into the doorway of Cleo's office. "Do you have a minute?"

"Oh, good gravy, *now* what?" She looked up from her memo with mild alarm. She thought she'd managed to smooth everything over.

She'd mollified Pastor Scott and Philomena and had seen them off—first him on the helicopter, and then her on the yacht. She'd made arrangements for Felicia Williams to borrow the speedboat for her emergency errand. And she'd apologized profusely to Eduardo Martinez for dragging him out to the island for no reason.

Was it too much to hope for a few uninterrupted minutes to actually do some work?

He laughed easily. "No fires to put out, I promise. Just a quick question."

She felt her mouth curve into a smile. "That's the best news I've had all day. What can I do for you?"

"I can't seem to find Lynette. I've looked everywhere. I checked with Mrs. Martin and your grand ... er, Mr. Santiago. They haven't seen her, and she didn't show up for lunch. Her meal is still in the refrigerator." A worry line creased his forehead.

"Oh! I've been so busy, I forgot."

She opened the long, shallow desk drawer where she kept her pens and pulled out a cream-colored envelope addressed to him. "Her niece showed up this morning. A surprise visit. She was in Miami for a legal conference, so she came down to take Lynette out to lunch. Lynette asked me to give this to you."

He pocketed the envelope. "Any idea when she'll be back?"

"Well, she said late afternoon. But the last time this attorney niece of hers took her out, they ended up in a lawyer bar in Little Havana, trading war stories and doing shots. We didn't see her for two days." She laughed at the memory.

He seemed less amused. "Okay, thanks."

"Is something wrong?"

"It seemed like she had something important to tell me. I wish I'd had a chance to talk to her before she left."

"Oh. Well, you were sort of busy doing God's work. If you hadn't calmed Detective Williams down, we might have had a real problem on our hands."

As far as she could tell, the possibilities had ranged from mayhem and bloodshed to Pastor Scott being hauled off in handcuffs. But somehow, no violence between law enforcement and the clergy had erupted in her facility. *Yet*.

"She's not going to forget what happened," he warned. "I can direct her energy to more productive matters for a while, but ..."

Cleo shrugged. "Pastor Scott's an adult. He'll have to deal with the consequences of his actions." As the words left her mouth, she wished she could grab them back. Despite her feelings about his behavior in the interview, it wasn't appropriate to exhibit such disloyalty.

"Speaking of consequences, do you have any plans to tell Mr. Santiago about your relationship?"

"Shhh." She jerked her head toward the hallway.

He got the hint and pulled the door closed behind him. "Sorry."

She felt self-conscious talking about her deepest secret with him, but, at the same time, she was desperate for someone to share her thinking with.

"I'm not sure yet whether or how to tell him. But I

certainly don't want him to find out through the well-oiled Golden Shores gossip machine. And I'd like to wait until this SUD cluster mess gets resolved. So get busy, would you?" She smiled to let him know she was mainly kidding.

"Fair enough. Hey, has that gossip machine spread anything about why Nurse Martinez was asking for extra shifts?"

She shook her head. "Nope. Nurse Mumma said she doesn't look gift horses in the mouth. He asked for extra nights, and she signed him up. End of story. I guess Detective Williams can ask him when she gets around to interviewing him."

"Hmm. Yeah, I suppose. Thanks for the note. I'll be in the storage closet with Mr. Gonzales's belongings if anyone's looking for me."

He turned to leave.

"Wait. Do you want me to find an orderly to help you take all that stuff to a reading room in the library? You'll be more comfortable."

"No, thanks. I want to disturb it as little as possible. But when you get a chance, can I look through Ms. Morales's things?"

"Oh, right." She removed a key from the ring on her desk. "This same key opens the closet we were in earlier and the one between the library and the reception area. Her belongings are in there."

She tossed the key in his direction, and he plucked it out of the air with two fingers.

"I'm not sure how long this will take ..."

"Keep it until you're done with it. I don't need access to either closet for anything."

"Thanks again. Don't work too hard."

She laughed helplessly and gestured at the paperwork piled up on her desk. "Right."

"And, Cleo, if you're waiting for the perfect time to talk to Mr. Santiago, remember this, *'What is past is left behind. The future is as yet unreached.'*"

She narrowed her eyes. "Is that a fancy way of saying there's no time like the present?'

He ducked his head and grinned. "Well, yeah, I guess it is."

"Noted. Have fun playing in the dirt."

CHAPTER TWENTY-SEVEN

Digging through Mr. Gonzales's dirt was decidedly *not* fun. Bodhi had scrounged up a metal chair from a stack in the library and had brought it into the closet. He'd cleared a spot on a shelf to use as a desk. Then he powered up his laptop and set his notepad and pencil beside it. With his temporary workspace arranged for maximum productivity, he got to work.

He found a package of blue exam gloves tucked into a pocket of his laptop bag and snapped them on. He dragged the cauldrons, heavy with dirt, from the center of the room to a spot on the side and moved the boxes to the space they'd occupied.

There were two stacks of four boxes each. Assuming they were all full, they held a considerable amount of stuff for a man living in a single room.

One by one, he removed the lid from each box and performed a visual survey of its contents. As Cleo had said, several of them contained dirt and assorted stuff—shards of glass and pottery, beads, branches, and coins. Odds and ends that he'd need to sort, categorize, and catalogue.

He found the loose bundle of bones in the sixth box. The skulls—some human, some not—were in the seventh box. But it was the eighth box that made his heart thump and his chest tighten. Several glass bottles of silver liquid lay in a nest of bubble wrap. More bottles, empty and uncorked, were scattered around the perimeter of the box. Shiny silver pools of liquid dotted the bottom of the box.

Elemental mercury. Liquid at room temperature. Silver. Poisonous.

He jammed the lid back onto the box and rocked back on his heels. What had Gonzales been doing with bottles full of highly toxic mercury?

"Bodhi? Are you in there?" Doctor Ashland's muffled voice came through the door followed by a knock.

Bodhi grabbed his computer, notes, and bag and opened the door.

"What are you doing in a closet? I thought Cleo was joking," Detective Williams said.

He pulled the door shut and locked it. Then he turned to face them.

Dr. Ashland studied his face. "You look like you've seen a ghost."

"Not a ghost. But something unsettling, for sure," Bodhi said as he regained control of his breath.

Detective Williams gestured to the handcart she was pulling. "We brought the equipment you wanted. Now what?"

Bodhi frowned. "I'm not sure. José Gonzales's personal belongings are in there."

Dr. Ashland nodded. "Great. So you want to bring them back to the lab to analyze?" He said it as if he wasn't quite sure.

And with good reason. Most medical examiners focused mainly on the corpse and left the artifacts, such as they were, to the forensic anthropologists. Bodhi had a sneaking suspicion no such creature was on staff in Dr. Ashland's shop.

"Well, I did. But along with a bunch of bones, some skulls, an assortment of debris and detritus, and some swords, there's a box full of elemental mercury in there."

"Oh." Dr. Ashland's eyes went round.

"Right. Oh," Bodhi agreed.

"Mercury, as in the stuff in a thermometer?"

Detective Williams asked.

"Yes."

"Isn't that toxic?"

"Yes," Bodhi and Dr. Ashland answered together.

"Oh."

They stared at one another in silence for a moment.

Then Bodhi said, "We'll leave it for now. The door's locked, and I have the key. We can think about what to do with it while we gather Ms. Morales's things. They're in a closet down the hall."

"Let's hope she doesn't have a box of anthrax," Detective Williams murmured.

He headed for the second closet with Dr. Ashland at his side. Detective Williams trailed them by several steps, pulling the handcart along behind her.

They reached the closet, and Bodhi dug the key out from his pants pocket. As he unlocked the door, he realized he was holding his breath.

He exhaled and flipped the light switch on the wall. He immediately noted three things. One, Esmerelda Morales had left behind far fewer belongings than had José Gonzales. Two, most of her possessions were articles of clothing, which hung from two metal racks in folds of silk, cotton, and polyester. And, three, while there was no evidence she'd collected dirt, there was ample evidence that she'd collected statues. Elaborate, colorful statues of saints stood in a neat row lined up on the top of a long wooden trunk and two hard-sided suitcases.

"Hmm."

"Hmm, what?" Detective Williams asked.

Bodhi started. He hadn't realized he'd made a noise.

"Oh. I'm surprised to see all the saints. Ms. Morales' friends were just telling me she hadn't been a particularly devout Catholic. I guess they underestimated her."

Detective Williams shook her head. "Santería. That's what it is—saint worship, literally."

He was getting the feeling he was in over his head. Then he remembered Lynette Johnson's unread note.

"Hang on." He pulled the envelope from his pocket and slit it open with a fingernail.

Bodhi,

My niece showed up for a visit, which is handy. She wants to take me to lunch, and I need to pick up a bottle of wine or two. Stop by later. We can raise a glass and I will tell you what you need to know about the palero.

Lyn

He refolded the note card and slipped it back into the envelope.

"Do either of you know what a *palero* is?"

Dr. Ashland shrugged. "Not me."

The color drained from Detective Williams's face. "Why?"

"I think Mr. Gonzales may have been one."

"You need to talk to Father Rafael," she answered in a shaky voice.

"Okay, after we catalogue Ms. Morales' things and decide what we're doing about the mercury and—"

"No. Now," she insisted. She turned to Dr. Ashland. "Joel, you can handle this, right?"

"Um, sure." His face was a study in bafflement.

"Give him the key," Detective Williams directed.

Bodhi handed it over. "I wouldn't go back in the other room."

"I'm not planning to, don't worry. I'll make some calls to the hazmat folks and see what they recommend. In the meantime, I'll photograph the items in here and write up an inventory. I have no idea what's going on, but it seems like good luck might be in order. So, good luck." Dr. Ashland gave him an encouraging smile.

"Let's go," Detective Williams said impatiently as she dragged him out into the hallway.

CHAPTER TWENTY-EIGHT

*Put on the whole armor of God, that
you may be able to stand against
the schemes of the devil.*

EPHESIANS 6:11

*Think not lightly of evil, saying, "It will
not come to me." Drop by drop is
the water pot filled.*

THE BUDDHA, DHAMMAPADA

Detective Williams commandeered Golden Shores' speedboat for the return trip to Big Pine Key. As the small boat cut through the waves, churning up spray, she shouted over the wind, "Maybe we should just take the boat straight to Key West. It'll be faster!"

Bodhi leaned in close to her ear so he could respond without yelling. "Whatever you're concerned about is clearly important, maybe even critically so. But there's no emergency here. Dock the boat in Golden Island's slip on Big Pine so Cleo doesn't report it stolen, please. A police chase on the open sea isn't going to get us to Father Rafael any sooner. You can slap your light on the top of your car and drive like a madwoman if you feel it's necessary."

"It probably is."

She was concentrating on piloting the boat and didn't turn to face him when she answered, but he could see that her expression was grim.

He fell silent until they reached the pier. They wriggled out of their life jackets and stowed them. Then Detective Williams handed the speedboat key to Golden Island's steward and sprinted toward the parking lot.

Bodhi followed behind at a deliberate pace. Not to slow her down, but because he knew she'd need to radio to dispatch and set up her light before she was ready to go. He reached the car just as she was ending her radio call.

"I asked dispatch to call ahead to Father Rafael

and let him know we're coming," she said as he buckled his seatbelt.

Before he could respond, she gunned the engine. The car lurched forward. She hit the lights but, thankfully, not the siren as she sped out of the lot and into the traffic traveling south on Route 1.

As they rocketed toward Key West, Bodhi took a moment to notice the blurred landscape outside the window.

"I don't have my land legs yet, so I guess if I get sick in your car it'll be seasickness, not carsickness," he said mildly.

She glanced at him as if to judge how serious he was. His face must have looked as green as he felt because she eased off the gas and reduced her speed.

"Sorry. But we need to talk to Father Rafael."

"I gathered that much, detective. Why don't you fill me in just a tiny bit so I can prepare for our discussion. What's a *palero?*"

She bit her lip and shook her head.

He tried another tack. "I know Father Rafael's not just a priest, he's a *santero*, too."

Her eyes went round. "You do? How?"

"Do you practice Santería?"

"No." She laughed at the thought.

"Then how did *you* know that about Father Rafael?"

"It's pretty much an open secret among certain people. I really am just a garden-variety Catholic. But Santería and Catholicism are closely intertwined where I grew up. Lots of my aunts and uncles follow both religions. It's all over the Keys. Those colorful, so-called novena candles in all the grocery stores are really Santería candles. And you can't walk through Miami without tripping over an offering to an *orisha*."

"An *orisha*?"

"A saint." She waved her hand in a helpless gesture. "Look, I'm really not qualified to explain it, but Father Rafael will be able to answer all your questions."

"Is that why we're going to see him?"

She didn't answer. She gripped the steering wheel so tightly her knuckles turned white.

"Felicia?"

She looked away from the road and met his eyes. "A *palero* is someone who practices Palo mayombe, Bodhi. It's the dark side of Santería. It's black magic. If Mr. Gonzales really was a *palero*, Father Rafael can help us."

CHAPTER TWENTY-NINE

The six o'clock bells were ringing when they pulled into the small lot behind Saint Lazarus's Shrine. As they stepped out of the car, Bodhi gazed up at the white stucco structure. It had a gabled teal and pink roof and was topped by a stained glass crucifix. It reminded him of the churches he'd seen in the Dominican Republic. It most certainly didn't look like a Catholic shrine in the United States.

"Is the architecture Cuban?"

Detective Williams craned her neck back and studied the building as if she were seeing it for the first time. She shrugged. "It's looks like a regular Floridian building to me."

As the last bell pealed, her stomach rumbled loudly. She gave Bodhi an embarrassed smile.

"Sorry. I just sort of realized I haven't eaten today. Have you?"

Bodhi rewound his day. "No. Actually, I haven't."

"Good. I know an authentic Cuban place. It's off the beaten path. Cheap. Good. And we'll be able to talk freely. Let's take Father Rafael out to dinner."

A small side door opened and a tall, dark-haired man wearing tailored black pants, a short-sleeved black dress shirt, and a white clerical collar stepped into view.

"Felicia!" He waved energetically, took the short set of stairs two at a time and, to Bodhi's surprise, swept Detective Williams into a hug.

"Father Rafael, this is Dr. Bodhi King." She smiled at the priest and gestured toward Bodhi.

"Bodhi, this is my cousin, Father Rafael Betancourt."

"Your cousin?" Bodhi echoed.

"Well, sorta cousin. His aunt is my aunt's sister-in-law. Is that right?"

"Close enough." The priest grasped Bodhi's hand with his right and covered it with his left. "I'm very happy to meet you, Dr. Bodhi King."

"Please, call me Bodhi, Father Rafael."

The priest smiled. His white teeth and his white

collar were stark and bright against his dark skin. "You're a Buddhist, Bodhi?"

"Yes, I am."

"Why don't you call me Rafael then, eh? Especially because I understand you want to talk about Santería." As he spoke, he carefully removed his collar and placed it in his pants pocket.

"If you like."

Detective Williams looped her arm through her cousin's elbow. "We haven't eaten. Can we take you to Tita's for rice and beans?"

Rafael smiled. "Always."

They walked a short distance. Detective Williams pointed out roosters and gypsy chickens. She was as relaxed as she'd been the first day on the yacht.

They stopped in front of an enormous gnarled tree. The thick, twisted trunk was massive, and the limbs reached toward the heavens.

"It's the kapok tree," Rafael explained. "They can grow to be well over one hundred feet. There's a sign around the corner that tells the history, the biology, and the mythology of the tree, if you're interested."

Bodhi was. So he stepped over the large roots snaking out of the ground and stood on the intersecting sidewalk. The sign detailed how the tree's large, foul-smelling, bell-shaped flowers opened once or twice a decade to be cross-pollinated by bats and explained the ancient Mayans' belief that the dead climbed a sacred kapok tree to reach heaven.

He rejoined the others, shaking his head. "What an amazing tree."

"It's a beautiful and awe-inspiring tree—a sign of God's hand in nature. But the thing I've always found funny about the sign is the mythology it leaves out." Rafael twisted his mouth into a wry smile.

"What's that?"

"The kapok tree is also found in Cuba. There, we call it the ceiba tree. It's venerated, maybe even worshipped, in Santería because the orishas and deities are believed to live in the branches. When someone is sick or dying, the sacrifice of a black-furred animal at the base of a ceiba is thought to pass on the animal's life to the ill one. And the Palo mayombe also worship the tree. They believe powerful spirits live in the tree. Bad spirits in some cases. So children in Cuba are warned by their parents to avoid the trees, not to play around them."

Bodhi looked up at the tree again. He could see how the imposing tree could be feared as well as revered.

"The duality of nature. Everything is both good

and bad." He fixed Rafael with a look. "It doesn't make for the most uplifting cultural marker reading, though."

Rafael chuckled.

Detective Williams clicked her tongue impatiently. "Are we finished looking at this blasted tree? I want to eat."

I t was never clear to Bodhi if Tita's was a licensed restaurant or if the *tita* in question was an actual aunt to Detective Williams, Rafael, or both.

He found himself in the front room of a small brick building tucked into a narrow, dusty alley patrolled by chickens. No sign hung in the window. No menus were handed out.

The tiny dining room was loud, dark, and crowded. Afro-Cuban jazz music played from a squat CD player balanced on a windowsill. The rice and beans were flavorful and plentiful. And the red table wine flowed freely.

His repeated requests for a glass of water were met with still more wine. Eventually, thirst won out.

Rafael seemed content to talk about music and

food and people whom Bodhi didn't know, but Detective Williams's earlier agitation returned in full force about an hour into the leisurely meal.

She leaned across the table. "Listen, this is serious. Bodhi thinks José Gonzales may have been a *palero*." Her drawn face looked haunted in the shadows thrown by the flickering candle in the center of the table.

"There's no maybe about it. He was a *palero*." Rafael wiped his mouth with his napkin.

"You knew? And you didn't do anything about it?"

"Leesh, tell me what could I do? Bryce Scott was reluctant to allow me to perform Catholic services in his temple to mammon. You think he was going to let me put on my *santero* robes and come in and do a protective ritual? Not that I didn't suggest it."

"I thought no one is supposed to know you practice Santería?" Bodhi furrowed his brow, puzzled.

"That's right, officially. The diocese would be ... displeased." He swept his arms around the room. "The community, they couldn't care less. The vast majority of my parishioners combine the two. But, that wouldn't fly in 99.9% of the churches in North America. And I understand that. So, when Cleo Clarkson called to see if I could perform an exorcism, I suggested they bring in a *santero*. If they'd agreed, I wouldn't have done it myself, of course. Tito Juan would have done it."

"Wait. Cleo Clarkson wanted you to perform an exorcism?" Detective Williams blinked at him.

"She was calling on Pastor Scott's behalf. Apparently, the residents were concerned that the building was under the control of demons. I explained that in the Catholic faith demonic possession happens to a *person*, not a structure, and that there are rules about exorcism."

He paused and sipped his wine before continuing. "Besides, my study group informed me that the rumors of Satanic possession were being spread by Pastor Scott's own lay ministers." He shook his head. "Julia Martin's grandson included. But, in a way they're not wrong."

"You believe there are evils spirits at Golden Shores?" Bodhi kept his voice neutral. He knew what it was to hold minority religious views. He had no intention of judging Rafael's beliefs, either as a priest or a *santero*.

"Let me explain Palo mayombe."

Bodhi lifted his glass. "Maybe a little more background on Santería would be helpful first."

Rafael nodded. "You understand that the word literally means 'Saint worship'? It has other names, especially in the Caribbean and in West Africa, but here, in the U.S., most people refer to it as Santería."

"I understand that it's a syncretization of Catholicism and another belief system, but I don't know anything about that other religion," Bodhi admitted.

"That's fair. Most practitioners of Santería here in Florida don't either. The two have become so closely mixed in Cuba that unwinding the strands is nearly impossible. West African slaves brought to the Caribbean and Latin America by the Spanish Empire, mainly those from parts of Nigeria, Benin, and Togo, practiced a religion called Yoruba. Yoruba spawned a host of syncretized religions. Santería is only one of many. But they have a lot in common."

"Detect—"

Detective Williams laughed. "At this point, and in this place, you might as well call me Felicia. Just don't make a habit of it."

He smiled. "Felicia said that Palo mayombe is the dark version of Santería."

Rafael tilted his head from one side to the other. "Eh, in broad strokes, sure."

"Well, excuse me. I'm not the religious scholar, now, am I?"

Her cousin went on as if she hadn't said anything. "Palo mayombe is viewed that way because, in Cuba and here, its practitioners have borrowed a lot of the

symbolism from Santeria. But, in fact, it did not origi-
nate from the region of West Africa sometimes called
Yorubaland. It traces its roots to the Congo basin in
Central Africa."

"So, Palo mayombe is a syncretized religion with
Santería?" Bodhi found himself wishing he had a pen
and paper.

"Not exactly. Followers of Santería don't appreciate the connection. Unlike the Roman Catholic
Church in Cuba, which recognizes Santería as a
cultural force, if nothing else, Santería wants nothing
at all to do with Palo mayombe."

"Can you speed this along a bit?" Felicia asked as a
smiling woman brought over a platter laden with
cafecito and flan.

Bodhi thanked the server and inhaled the rich
aroma of the Cuban coffee while the cousins bickered
softly. Between the heaping portions of arroz congri,
the plate of plantains, the wine, and now coffee and
dessert, he was feeling more decadent than he had
in years.

Apparently, Felicia and Rafael came to some reso-
lution while he was savoring a mouthful of flan.

Rafael caught Bodhi's eyes. "Here's the deal.
Leesh says I have until she finishes her dessert and

coffee to give background. Then we need to deal with the actual issue at hand. So, I'm going to talk fast and gloss over a lot. Like Christianity, Santería is monotheistic. Just as in Christianity, there's a Trinity. Instead of Father, Son, and Holy Spirit, it's Olodumare, Olofi, and Olorun. With me?"

"Yes."

"Good. The orishas are the functional equivalent of the Catholic saints. In fact, that's really how the two religions became intertwined. The West African slaves noticed the saints that their Catholic owners prayed to and honored bore a strong resemblance to their orishas. It's important to note here that neither religion really 'worships' the saint/orisha. You worship God. You venerate the saints/orishas." He paused. "I don't know how any of this equates to Buddhism."

Bodhi shook his head. "It doesn't. But I'm following you. My neighbor prays to Saint Anthony when she can't find her glasses."

"Yes! Saint Anthony's orisha counterpart would be Elegguá, for instance. Each orisha was assigned a saint, so that the slaves could pray to them without detection."

Bodhi pictured the row of statues that Esmerelda Morales had owned. "So, when Ms. Morales prayed to Saint Anthony was she really praying to Elegguá?"

"No. She was praying to both of them."

"Okay."

Felicia raised her eyebrows at how easily he accepted this duality, but he figured this was one area in which having no preconceived understanding was an advantage.

"Now, the folks you met at Golden Shores, they all had"—he reverted to Catholicism here and made the sign of the cross when he mentioned his deceased parishioners—"or have a special affinity for the orisha Babalú Ayé, who we call San Lázaro or Saint Lazarus. Do you know the story of Lazarus?"

Bodhi squinted as he tried to remember. "Jesus brought him back from the dead."

"Excellent! So that Lazarus is Lazarus of Bethany. There's also a parable in Luke about a leper, who some people believe is Lazarus of Bethany and some people believe is a different man. Doesn't matter. The important part is that sick or infirm Cuban Catholics pray to San Lázaro for healing, and practitioners of Santería pray to Babalú Ayé for the same miracle. These two in particular are very tightly connected. There's a big festival every year for Saint Lazarus in Cuba, and it's very much a Santería event. There's a famous shrine to him there, which much like my old parish openly accepts Santería."

"And now you're at Saint Lazarus's Shrine here."

Rafael smiled. "Bingo. So, the social club would pray to San Lázaro—and other orishas, as needed—but he's our guy, so to speak. They would light candles and leave offerings to him—fruit, flowers, what have you."

"Animal sacrifices?" Bodhi asked.

"No. Not at Golden Shores. Too risky."

"But Mr. Gonzales had bones and bits of feathers and fur among his rather bizarre belongings. Along with skulls—at least one of which might be a human cranium. So what's that about?"

"Palo mayombe doesn't recognize the orishas. *Paleros* appeal to the forces of nature. Animal sacrifice is much more common. So is ritual blood-letting and the use of human remains. It sounds like you found his *nganga*."

"Is a *nganga* a cauldron filled with dirt, sticks, and stuff?"

"Nailed it."

"He had two—a big one and a little one. And a tower of boxes filled with more sticks, coins, swords, shells, beads, and bones, among other things."

"These items are in boxes?"

"Yes, filled with more dirt."

Rafael groaned. "That's a big problem. A *palero*'s

cauldron is sacred. It's the source of his power. Now I'm not an expert, but I believe the cauldron is also where the spirits of the Dead are thought to reside. A human skull is placed in the cauldron for the spirits, to give them intelligence."

"This cranium was definitely in a box. A white box from the paper supply store," Bodhi informed him.

"So, here's the thing. The *nganga* typically is used for destructive purposes. To work curses or in a criminal enterprise—never anything positive. The belief is that once the *palero* dies, *his* spirit is bound with the cauldron, increasing its power. There are very specific, secret rituals for the disassembly of a cauldron. I think it has to be taken apart in a certain way and buried—I'm not sure. But I do know it's not supposed to be dumped into a bunch of boxes from the local office store and stuck in a closet."

Felicia pushed her empty flan dish forward. "Time's up. But Bodhi, you forgot to ask him about the mercury."

He'd been so rapt, he'd managed to forget the bottles of poison rattling around in one of Mr. Gonzales's boxes. "Right. Would a *palero* use elemental mercury in his work?"

Rafael nodded. "He would. I don't know the

details, but the most common rituals in which mercury would be used are those to bring luck, love, or money or to ward off evil. I think the Palo mayombe practitioners may also use it to divine the future. It always seemed awfully risky to me."

Another thought occurred to Bodhi. "How did the social club learn that Mr. Gonzales was a *palero?*"

Rafael sighed philosophically. "Ah, there are signs that they'd notice. The beads. The clothing. Ritual scratches on his body. And he, of course, knew what those statues of the saints in their rooms really were. Tensions simmered under the surface for a while. But I believe he made a play for Esmerelda, and Carlos reacted. That's when things got really heated. He threatened to rat them out to Ms. Clarkson. Mr. Ruiz, the first of my parishioners to die, apparently confronted him in the locker room after a swim, and Mr. Gonzales cursed him."

Again with the curses. Bodhi opened his mouth to ask his next question, but at that moment, the sound of three ringtones interrupted the jazz music. He looked down at his ringing and vibrating pocket and noticed out of his peripheral vision that Rafael and Felicia were doing the same.

As the words Cleo Clarkson was saying registered

in his brain, he could tell from the way Felicia drew back in shock and Rafael lowered his head in sorrow that their callers were delivering the same news:

Lynette Johnson had just been found dead—laying in her bed with a look of horror frozen on her face.

CHAPTER THIRTY

The drive north was quick. And, for several long miles, quiet.

Bodhi had insisted on giving the front passenger seat to Father Rafael. But neither of Felicia's passengers was in a talkative mood.

The camaraderie the three of them had enjoyed at Tita's had shattered with the ringing cell phones, and the stress level in the car made Felicia feel as if she were choking.

She glanced at her cousin, who appeared to be praying in the seat beside her. His white collar was back in place and he sat with his head bowed and his eyes closed. His lips were moving, but he made no sound.

Her eyes drifted up to the rearview mirror and she checked on Bodhi. He appeared to be meditating. His head was unbent and his eyes were closed. His hands rested on his thighs and his forefingers and thumbs met in two ovals. His lips were not moving, but she could have sworn she heard a vibrating sound coming from his throat.

Unable to pray or meditate, she found solace by zipping up the mostly deserted stretches of highway, imagining the car was a bird.

Bodhi broke the silence. "Cleo said Lynette came back from her outing with her niece around seven o'clock and begged off dinner and board games. She said she was beat."

"Dr. Ashland wanted me to tell you that the body ... she ... was still warm when Ed called him to her side." The piece of information had fallen out of her head almost as soon as Joel had shared it. Felicia scolded herself—this was no time to lose focus.

"Eduardo Martinez found her?'

"Yes," Felicia answered miserably. "The only saving grace will be if those two sycophantic aides are also working."

Bodhi said nothing, but she thought she heard a hitch in his breath.

"What?" she demanded.

"They're not working tonight. Cleo gave Charlene

and Philomena both the night off because of their, uh, experience today."

Their experience. What he meant by that, she knew full well, was the unpleasant witness interviews where she'd blown up at Pastor Scott.

Great. Another thing she could berate herself over. Her quick temper was going to result in even more suspicion being cast on Ed.

She swore under her breath.

Father Rafael opened his eyes. "Are you okay?"

"I'm fine." She regretted the terseness of her tone instantly, but neither Father Rafael nor Bodhi pressed her on her obvious lie.

"How did Mr. Santiago sound when he called you?" Bodhi asked the priest.

Father Rafael considered his answer for a moment. "He sounded mournful, but not at all surprised. Julia's not handling it well, though. Hector said he was going to call her grandson and ask him to come out to be with her. She's terribly anxious about yet another death, and, of course, Lynette was one of her closest friends."

"Another death from within the circle of Santería practitioners has me feeling pretty anxious, myself," Bodhi admitted.

"Amen."

Felicia blinked. "You two don't seriously think the ghost of Mr. Gonzales or his evil spirit or a bunch of bones sitting in a boxful of dirt killed them. Or do you?"

She got no response. Then after a moment, Bodhi said, "I liked her."

"She was a likable woman, wasn't she? And such stories." Father Rafael laughed softly at some memory.

Felicia pulled into the parking lot at the dock. She could see the yacht tied up and bobbing in its slip. The lights were on and the engine was already running. The captain must have been told to be ready for them.

Not until she'd run across the lot and onto the boat did she realize that Pastor Scott and his blonde assistant were aboard. She hesitated, but the pastor acted as though she weren't even there.

She took a life jacket from the pile in the assistant's arms and slipped into it wordlessly.

Bodhi and Father Rafael followed a moment later and claimed jackets of their own. They sat, one on each side of her, and nodded to Pastor Bryce in silent greeting.

The five of them looked at one another and waited for the boat to leave the slip.

After a moment or two of inactivity, Pastor Scott called to the steward, "What's the hold up?"

"Sorry, sir. Ms. Clarkson told us there'd be six passengers. We're waiting for an Arthur Lopez."

Felicia watched as the pastor's head snapped back. "You're taking your orders from Ms. Clarkson now?"

The man ducked his head and said apologetically, "She runs Golden Shores, sir. As far as I know, they own this vessel."

Felicia passed the time as they awaited their sixth man watching the pastor's face turn varying shades of purple. It occurred to her that hidden inside every tragedy was the seed of a comedy.

CHAPTER THIRTY-ONE

_____

Golden Shores was in an uproar. Actually, Bodhi thought, uproar might be too mild a descriptor. It had descended into sheer chaos—helped in no small part, he was sure, by the arrival of the yacht and its six passengers. The building buzzed with activity.

Dr. Ashland pulled Bodhi aside. "Let me fill you in quickly, okay? Then I need to find Felicia."

Detective Williams appeared behind him. "You found me. What's going on, Joel?"

Dr. Ashland tugged on his earlobe. "It's a helluva thing. I catalogued everything in Ms. Morales's closet. So I figured I'd put on a mask and get started on Mr. Gonzales's mess. I made pretty good progress, too. I even called out the hazmat crew and had that mercury taken out of here safely. I was just getting busy with those bones when Cleo came racing in."

"What time was this?"

"Around nine. When the nurses rounded at eight o'clock for the shift change, Mrs. Johnson was sleeping. Chef Tonga had the kitchen crew send her dinner up when they were cleaning up for the evening. Which, by the way, there goes your copper poisoning theory. She wasn't eating his cooking."

"I know, believe me. I already thought of that. I guess the chef can go back to cooking in his shiny copper pots and pans."

"Anyway, Nurse Martinez took her dinner into her when he passed out sleeping meds at nine o'clock. That's when he found her."

Felicia shook her head. "What are the odds?"

Dr. Ashland and Bodhi exchanged a look. The medical examiner's expression seemed to say *you talk to her*.

"Detective Williams, I know you don't think Eduardo Martinez has anything to do with these deaths, but at this point, you've got to interview him." Bodhi said it as gently as he could then braced himself for the explosion.

But it never came.

"I know," she sighed. "I'll talk to him while you

two take care of Mrs. Johnson's body. Father Rafael's in there now, though. Can you give him a little bit of time?"

"Sure."

"Of course."

"Thanks." She managed a wan smile before she turned and trudged down the hall.

Dr. Ashland and Bodhi watched her walk away. Then Dr. Ashland said, "Are you comfortable if I leave you here and get back to the office? I want to get Mr. Gonzales's things put away before Lynette's body comes in."

Bodhi hesitated. "Of course. But you should know … apparently all that stuff has religious significance." He didn't know how to explain about the *nganga*. But it made him uneasy to send Dr. Ashland off to mess around with a *palero*'s altar and religious items.

Dr. Ashland screwed up his face. "Really? I thought folks confirmed it's not Santería."

"It's not. It's some dark magico-religious system."

The medical examiner sighed. "Well, that ship has sailed. His altar or whatever it was has already been disturbed. I just want to examine those long bones and skulls. There's some trace blood, too. I'll photograph everything before I move anything."

"I guess that's all you can do."

They looked at each other for a moment, both thinking the same thought. It was nights like these that made forensic pathology worthwhile. Sure, neither of them would get much—if any—sleep. But this was what they were meant to do: dig into the messy business of death and make sense of it.

Cleo's eyes were dry but rimmed with red.

"Did you speak to Lynette when she got back?" Bodhi asked gently.

She nodded. "I ran into her in the hallway. She was in a great mood. She had one of those fancy cloth wine totes from a wine shop in Miami. She invited me to join her for a nightcap after I finished up for the evening." Her voice broke.

"How are Hector and Julia holding up?"

"Not great. Mrs. Martin's grandson Arthur is here for her. But poor Mr. Santiago has no one."

Bodhi held her gaze.

She looked away and mumbled, "I can't. Not now."

"I'm sure Father Rafael is comforting him."

She nodded. "Will Nurse Martinez be arrested?"

"I honestly don't know. That's not my area of

expertise, but I imagine he'll at least be taken down to the station to be interviewed formally."

Her chin jutted out. "Okay, good."

"I don't think he had anything to do with the deaths, Cleo."

"Maybe not. But people feel unsafe. We have to do *something*. And Pastor Scott wants to fire him right now. I'm going to at least put him on unpaid leave until this gets sorted out."

Father Rafael appeared in the doorway with his mouth turned down into a frown. "I hate to interrupt, but we have an issue. Two, really. Lynette's niece is here and she says something's missing from her room— two bottles of wine, to be exact. And Julia Martin is reporting that a novena candle has gone missing from her room."

A shadow of irritation glanced across Cleo's face. It moved so quickly, Bodhi almost thought he'd imagined it.

"Father, this really isn't the time. I'm sorry to hear that, but at the moment we're dealing with yet another death and—"

"And your guests feel unsafe and vulnerable. It would help if they could at least have some security in their personal space."

She closed her eyes and her long lashes brushed

her cheeks. "Of course, Father Rafael. You're right. Forgive me."

She stood and addressed Bodhi. "If you'll excuse me. I need to talk to Nurse Mumma about these petty thefts."

She walked out of the room as if she were weighted down with a boulder. Father Rafael smiled encouragingly when she passed by.

As soon as she was out of earshot, he turned to Bodhi and said, "The wine and the candle were both for personal protection rituals. Julia is beside herself. And I can't say I blame her."

"Golden Shores is going to suspend Eduardo Martinez pending an investigation. Maybe you should let Detective Williams know about the missing items?"

"I will. What are you going to do?"

"I'm going to sit with Lynette's body if it's okay with her niece."

He'd been putting off seeing her since they'd arrived at Golden Shores. But he knew avoidance wasn't healthy. He had to face her corpse.

He pushed himself to his feet feeling very tired.

"Oh, Rafael?"

"Yes?"

"The disassembled altar is currently sitting in the

medical examiner's office—the cauldron, the boxes of dirt, and the rest. What should we do with it when we're done?"

The priest's eyes were round and concerned. "I honestly don't know. But I'll pray on it."

CHAPTER THIRTY-TWO

Felicia had to restrain herself from hugging her person of interest. Ed looked so dejected and beaten down, she wanted to cry.

"Leesh, I don't know what's happening to these people. I'll swear on a stack of Bibles." His tone and his eyes implored her to believe him.

The problem was that she *did* believe him. But that wasn't enough. It would be reckless not to take a hard look at him. Six people had died during his shifts.

There was a soft knock at the door. She gave Ed a look that said *don't even think about moving*, then rose to answer the door. She opened it a crack and glared through the opening.

"What?"

Bodhi looked back at her impassively.

"Oh, it's you." She yanked the door open and waved him in.

"Are you taking Nurse Martinez to the police station?"

"I have to. For his sake and mine, I'm going to need to have the interview videotaped."

"Can I ask him a few questions about Mr. Gonzales before you go? You can stay and listen."

"Sure. Knock yourself out. I'm actually going to make a few calls and arrange for a ride for you and Father Rafael."

"Don't worry about me. I'll figure something out," Bodhi assured her.

"Nah, that's one of the few perks of being a parish priest, people trip all over themselves to do you favors. I can scare up someone who wants to get in good with the Big Guy."

Before she left, she turned and crouched beside Ed's chair. "You're one of my oldest friends, but we're going to have to do this completely by the book. Dr. King is probably your best shot at getting clear of this, so tell him what he wants to know. Got it?"

"I got it."

As she stood, a thought struck her. "One question, though: why did you request those extra shifts? I thought Marisole was giving you a hard time about working nights."

"She is. But that's because she's so tired. She's pregnant again and chasing after Little Eddie wears her out. But, also, she's pregnant again and a two-bedroom, one-bath apartment isn't going to cut it for long. I wanted to crush my hours for the next six months and get together a deposit on a townhouse."

Her heart sank. "Congratulations to you and Mari."

He couldn't even muster up a smile. "Thanks. It's a terrible time to be suspended without pay."

She nodded and hurried from the room before she either burst into tears or punched her fist through a wall.

"I just have a few questions," Bodhi promised as he sat down across from the miserable-looking nurse.

"Okay."

"I've been trying to tie together the five—now six—deaths. To figure out how they all fit into the same pattern. But I'm starting to think they don't."

Eduardo Martinez pulled a face that suggested he

didn't think much of the vaunted death cluster expert. "Why would you say that?"

"Well, socially, Mr. Gonzales wasn't close with any of the others, all of whom were close with one another. So, right there, he doesn't fit the pattern."

"That's because José Gonzales wasn't tight with any of the other residents. If you want to know the truth, he was a pretty nasty guy all round."

Bodhi nodded. "And he wasn't a practicing Catholic, correct?"

"As far as I know, he never went to any church services. He didn't participate in any other activities either, though. He spent most of his time alone in his room with the door closed."

"Did he have any hobbies or interests?"

The nurse scrunched up his face in concentration. "Aside from making his dolls, I don't think so."

"He made dolls?"

Eduardo barked out a short laugh. "They weren't anything fancy. They were little clothespin people— and they were kind of sloppy-looking. But he had a whole drawer full of them. Kind of an unusual hobby, but to each his own."

Bodhi pictured the handful of dolls strewn around a box of dirt. "You're sure it was a whole drawer? Could you estimate how many?"

Eduardo threw his hands up in the air. "Three dozen? Four dozen? A lot."

"Did you notice any changes in his demeanor in the days and weeks leading up to his death?"

Eduardo cocked his head to the right and pursed his lips. After a moment, he said, "I guess I'd say there was a change in intensity, but not in kind. I mean, he was an unpleasant person. But the last week or so, he was all amped up, ranting about his enemies."

"Was he lucid?"

"Sometimes. But sometimes he just went off. He'd get so mad, he'd start shaking."

"Are you sure he was shaking from anger? Could he have been having tremors?"

"Could have been," Eduardo answered slowly. "He didn't have a history of tremors, though."

"Did he have any chronic health conditions?"

"Halitosis."

"Pardon?"

"Halitosis, gingivitis, whatever you want to call it. His breath was fierce."

"Was it always that way—his breath?"

"Actually, I'm not sure. I never got that close to him until I found him dead. But his breath about knocked me out when I leaned in to check for a pulse."

Bodhi turned this over in his mind. "Did he have any visitors?"

"Just one. This really jacked young dude with a shaved head and lots of tribal-looking tattoos. He called Mr. Gonzales his godfather. When Mr. Gonzales died, Ms. Clarkson asked me to call the guy to come in and clear out his stuff."

"He never did. Did you speak to him or leave a message—if you remember?"

Eduardo nodded slowly. "I definitely remember because it was weird. A woman answered and said that the godson couldn't come in and claim the belongings because he was in the hospital."

"Did she say why?"

"Yeah. Mercury poisoning."

Bryce reminded himself that two men of God should be able to have a difference of opinion without a loss of civility. He knew this to be true, but his patience was thin.

It had been an exceedingly long day, beginning with his confrontation with Detective Williams. The news that yet another resident had died had not improved matters. And the disagreement with Cleo as to how to deal with Nurse Martinez cemented his dark mood.

And now this Catholic priest was imploring him to ... do what exactly?

"Father Rafael, maybe I'm misunderstanding. I thought you told Cleo that the Church wouldn't authorize you to perform an exorcism?"

"That's right, Pastor Scott."

"So what is this rite you're proposing?" Was rite the right word, or was it ritual? He wasn't even sure.

Father Rafael twisted his mouth to one side and thought. "I'm afraid I don't know the appropriate analogue. Does your church have any ceremonies that laypeople perform?"

"Ceremonies? No."

The priest tried again. "Do you remember when you and I talked about how important the prayer cards and statues of the saints are to my congregants?"

Of course he did. "Yes. And the rosaries and the other trappings of your religion."

"It would give the Catholic residents—some of them, at least, some comfort to be able to pray to the saints for protection. Simply leave an offering in front of a statue, recite a prayer. It's harmless." He flashed a bright smile.

"It's idolatry."

"Pastor Scott, respectfully, it's not."

Bryce shook his head. "The answer is no. I'm too tired to engage in a theological debate with you. But if your flock needs more security than you can provide, then perhaps they should consider one of my services. At Golden Island, Father Rafael, we worship the Lord, not some statue."

Father Rafael closed his eyes for a fraction of a second then nodded. "Good night, Pastor Scott."

He let himself out of the conference room Bryce had commandeered.

"May God bless you," Bryce called after him.

The priest didn't respond. At least, he didn't respond directly, but Bryce heard him muttering under his breath something that sounded suspiciously like, "You worship money, not the Lord."

CHAPTER THIRTY-THREE

When you hear hoofbeats, think of horses not zebras.

DR. THEODORE WOODWARD,
UNIVERSITY OF MARYLAND
SCHOOL OF MEDICINE

Horses, *not zebras.* The aphorism galloped through Bodhi's mind in a loop. As soon as Father Rafael's friend dropped him at the medical examiner's office, he powered up his laptop to look for a horse.

Dr. Ashland was in the autopsy room. Bodhi knocked on the door and waved at him through the small window. The medical examiner nodded. A few moments later, he came out into the hall and pulled down his mask.

"What's up? I'm just finishing up with the bones and skulls so I can clean the place up before Lynette Johnson's body arrives."

"Mr. Gonzales had one frequent visitor, a godson. He was recently hospitalized with mercury poisoning. And Father Rafael said a *palero* like Mr. Gonzales would use mercury in his rituals."

"You think they were working together?"

"Could have been."

Dr. Ashland nodded. "Some of the stones and shards of pottery and other crap in those boxes had been coated with mercury, too. There were globules clinging to some of those finger puppets or dolls or whatever they are. And I guess this is the part where I make your night."

"Please do."

"I may have mentioned that the toxicology lab has a four-to-six week turnaround time on testing results. Well, it's been five weeks since Mr. Gonzales died. Guess what was waiting in my email in-box when I got back tonight?"

"And?"

"Good thing we didn't spring for genetic testing for Wilson disease—there was no evidence of copper accumulation. But there were elevated blood mercury levels."

"How elevated?"

"Five hundred micrograms per liter."

"Isn't background level something like ten micrograms?"

"It's ten, precisely. He had fifty times that. I checked—assuming chronic exposure—five hundred could result in neuropsychiatric and central nervous system effects and the early stage renal problems. But his kidneys were okay."

Bodhi mentally ticked off the symptoms that Eduardo Martinez had listed: explosiveness; irritability; introversion; tremors; and halitosis.

"Isn't bad breath also a symptom?"

"It is."

"So, Mr. Gonzales suffered from chronic elemental mercury exposure. Did it kill him?"

"It likely contributed. There's also a chance he had an acute exposure at some point in the days leading up to his death, say a spill. With the body burden he was already carrying, that could have sent him over the edge."

Dr. Ashland's hypothesis was a decent one. "Could've," Bodhi agreed.

"We could exhume him and x-ray him. Literature

suggests radio-opaque lines can form in the long bones, but even if we confirmed mercury poisoning, that wouldn't establish it as the cause of death.

"No, it wouldn't."

"And there's still the matter of the other five deaths. And the rictus grin."

"I'm working on a theory about that right now."

"Oh? Can I get a hint?"

"We've been looking for a zebra. I think there may be a much simpler explanation, at least, for the five Catholic/Santerians. And maybe even for Mr. Gonzales."

Dr. Ashland waited with an expectant air.

"I have some research to do. But I think they were scared to death."

The medical examiner cocked his head. "You mean, literally?"

"Yes. I think they believed they would die, and so they did."

Dr. Ashland blinked a few times. "Well."

"I know."

"At this point, Bodhi, I'd believe just about anything. You go do your research while I finish up in here. I should be able to find some teabags around here somewhere. I'll fire up the coffee pot and microwave you some hot water, and we'll get this party started."

CHAPTER THIRTY-FOUR

*Your worst enemy cannot harm you
as much as your own thoughts,
unguarded.*

THE BUDDHA, DHAMMAPADA

*Yea, though I walk through the valley of
the shadow of death, I will fear
no evil.*

PSALM 23:4

Bodhi hit the button to start the coffee brewing for his host then let himself out of Joel Ashland's camper as quietly as he could.

As he walked to the water's edge, his eyes burned from exhaustion. But otherwise, physically and mentally, he felt okay. He'd have to remember to let Sasha know her planned nap tactic worked.

A workaholic attorney friend had once told him that the secret to an all-nighter was taking a ninety-minute nap at some point between one and three o'clock in the morning. Of course, she also recommended the copious consumption of coffee. Joel had chosen that tried and true method. He was now crashing and, judging by the rattling noise coming from the back of his Airstream, snoring heavily.

Bodhi settled on the bench and watched the waves dance. As he did, he formulated his plan. First, he needed to assemble his team—Joel, Cleo, Detective Williams, and Rafael. Second, he needed to convince them that Mr. Ruiz, Mr. Caldron, Mr. Garcia, Ms. Morales, and Lynette Johnson had died of fright. Third, he had to explain what they were going to do about it.

He considered that forensic pathology typically

didn't include a 'meting out justice' component. But, in this case, he'd make an exception.

With the plan fixed in his mind, he meditated on it before returning to Joel's place.

When he eased the door open and walked in, the medical examiner was banging around the kitchenette, literally.

"Everything okay?" Bodhi asked as Dr. Ashland slammed a cabinet closed.

"You tell me. I just got a call from some lawyer for Golden Island Church. You're banned from the property. And they're refusing to release Lynette Johnson's body."

Bodhi did a quick calculation. "It's okay. It doesn't matter."

Dr. Ashland's jaw hinged open. "It doesn't matter? Of course it matters."

"Not really. They can't ban Detective Williams from the island, can they?"

"Well ... no." He narrowed his eyes. The heavy bags that had taken up residence beneath his eyes during the night seemed to swallow them whole. "What are you driving at?"

"I figured out what's causing the deaths at Golden Shores, and I think I know how to stop them. But we're going to need help. Is Mangrove Mama's open for breakfast?"

"Sure."

"Will you call Detective Williams and ask her to meet us there? Tell her to bring Father Rafael. I'll call Cleo. She can bring Arthur Lopez."

After everyone had placed a breakfast order, the waiter disappeared into the kitchen, and Bodhi looked around the table.

"Thanks for coming. Dr. Ashland and I wanted to let this group know what we've learned, and getting everyone together seemed to be the most efficient way to do that."

"Why are *they* here?" Detective Williams asked, throwing Cleo and Arthur a dark look.

Arthur nodded, as if he was wondering the same thing.

"For the same reason Father Rafael is here. They both care deeply about the surviving Santería practitioners."

"Maybe Arthur does. After all, Mrs. Martin is his grandmother. But it's just a job for her, even if she does call the residents 'guests,'" Detective Williams retorted.

"No, it's more than that," Cleo said softly.

The detective snorted.

"Mr. Santiago's my grandfather." Cleo made the announcement to her placemat.

After a long silence, Father Rafael leaned forward. "He is? He told me he had only one son, who died of a drug overdose years ago."

Cleo raised her eyes. "Yes, Henry Santiago was my biological father. Before he died, he got a drug-addicted prostitute pregnant. She carried me to term then left me in the hospital nursery and walked out without looking back. I was adopted by a couple who ran a fishing charter out of Key Largo. They knew her name from the hospital records, and I was able to piece the rest together after I turned eighteen. I'm sure Mr. Santiago has no idea that he has a granddaughter. Any other questions?" She lifted her chin and delivered the words as a challenge.

Even Detective Williams was silenced by her story, so Bodhi continued. "The death cluster didn't begin with Mr. Gonzales. It began with Mr. Ruiz. Dr. Ashland?"

"Mr. Gonzales was suffering from chronic mercury poisoning, and it appears he may also have had an acute mercury exposure in the days leading up to his death," Dr. Ashland explained.

"Did he eat too much fish?" Cleo asked.

"Not that kind of mercury. Elemental mercury, which some people call quicksilver or liquid silver," Bodhi explained.

Father Rafael jumped in. "Mr. Gonzales was a *palero*, a practitioner of Palo mayombe. Mercury is used in Palo mayombe spells and rituals."

"And Mr. Gonzales had several bottles of it in his room," Bodhi added.

Cleo gasped. "That's what killed everyone— mercury poisoning?"

"No. That's what killed Mr. Gonzales. I believe the others were literally scared to death."

The arrival of the waiter with a tray of coffees, juices, and waters prevented anyone from voicing a reaction to his bombshell, but he could tell they'd need some convincing.

When the waiter left, Bodhi wasted no time trying to explain, "I got caught up looking for a medical explanation of the rictus grin, an expression that mimics terror. But the people who died didn't have the rictus grin. They were actually terrified when they died."

"Wait—including Mr. Gonzales?" Detective Williams asked.

"That's our working hypothesis. If he knew he was dying, and he probably did—acute mercury poisoning isn't an easy way to go— are there specific things he should have done beforehand, as a *palero*?" Bodhi directed the question to Father Rafael.

"Yes. He would need to make arrangements for his altar and his cauldron. It would have weighed on his mind if he failed to do so. It's very serious business. When a *palero* dies, his godson or goddaughter, an initiate who's bound to him through his cauldron, handles a farewell ceremony for the practitioner and, generally, either inherits his *nganga* or ritualistically destroys it. It's a big deal." The priest's somber tone matched his facial expression.

"So if his godson was in the hospital and unable to come before he died, would he be worried about dying without making the proper arrangements?"

"Terrified."

"Wait, do *you* practice Palo mayombe, too?" Arthur blurted.

"No. Palo mayombe is antithetical to the Roman Catholic belief system and my personal beliefs. It's a dark, evil practice," the priest assured him.

He glanced at Cleo before continuing to explain to Arthur, "As I'm sure your grandmother's told you, I am a *santero*, a Santerían priest, as well as a Catholic priest."

"Actually, she never mentioned it," Arthur mumbled. "But I know she practices it."

"She does?" Cleo's eyes went wide. "Wait, the social club?"

"All of them," Bodhi confirmed. "They were— and, in the case of your grandfather and Arthur's grandmother, are—Catholics who also practice Santería."

"But ..."

"It's really not as uncommon as you might think," Father Rafael assured her.

Plates of eggs, French toast, and pancakes arrived. Bodhi sipped his water and waited until the others had salted, syruped, and buttered their breakfasts to their liking.

Then he dove right back in. "Mr. Gonzales was targeting the six of them. There was at least one confrontation between him and a member of the group, and he cursed them all."

"When you say cursed, you mean wished death on them?" Detective Williams asked around a mouthful of eggs.

"Yes."

"You're saying he killed them using black magic?" Arthur's skepticism was painted all over his face.

"No. His curse killed them because they believed it would. As I said at the outset, they died of fright."

"Okay, sure, we've all read *The Hound of the Baskervilles*, but outside a Sherlock Holmes mystery, is that really possible?" Father Rafael asked.

"It is. Numerous research papers have been published on the phenomenon. The earliest I found was from the 1940s. A researcher proposed that people who died from what he called voodoo death experienced shock after being cursed with death. In the seventy-five years or so since the publication of that paper, science has proved, many times over, that the emotions and the body are linked. When a person believes he's in danger, there's an immediate hormonal stress response. A cascade of hormones and nerve chemicals is released by the brain. Under the right circumstances, this stress response could result in sudden cardiac death."

"You believe these conditions existed at Golden Shores?" Detective Williams asked.

"Yes. So, whether you're Sir Charles Baskerville encountering a hellhound on a foggy moor or a poor sap on the receiving end of a voodoo curse, you have to believe the event could kill you for this to happen."

Bodhi surveyed the faces around the table to make sure everyone was still with him. "If you're a person who believes in the dark power of Palo mayombe, and you've been cursed by a *palero*, you're going to believe that curse can kill you."

"Maybe, but ..." Cleo seemed skeptical.

"This part's also borne out by science. There's a condition called tetraphobia, which is fear of the number four."

"Of course there is," Detective Williams muttered caustically.

"Just eat your bacon and hear him out," Father Rafael chided her.

"In Japanese and Chinese, the word for the number four and the word for death sound very similar. So, much like the West considers thirteen to be an unlucky number, many Asian cultures view four as an unlucky number. So researchers examined over two hundred thousand death certificates of Japanese-Americans and Chinese-Americans and compared them to death certificates of Caucasian Americans. They found a pronounced fourth-day peak in cardiac deaths of the Asian-Americans, but not of the Caucasians. Significantly more Asian-Americans died from heart attacks on the fourth day of the month than any other day of a given month. And the effect was bigger in places that had cohesive Asian cultural centers."

"But how?" Arthur put down his fork and wrinkled his forehead.

"The hypothesis, and I think it's a good one, is that if you live in, say, Chinatown, and you're ingrained in Chinese culture, everyone around you is stressed out on the fourth of the month, because four's unlucky. Your stress is amplified by the stress and anxiety of the people around you and, boom, here comes the body's hormonal stress response again."

"So, my *lita* and her friends were scared when Mr. Gonzales cursed them. Then he died, and they knew that made him more powerful. So they got more stressed out, and then one of them died. And ..."

"And every time one of them dies, it increases the fear factor for the survivors," Cleo finished.

"Right. But there's another piece. I found a paper about a death cluster of Hmong immigrants. One hundred and seventeen men died of SUNDS."

"Do you mean SUD?"

Bodhi smiled at the detective's question. "Nope, as it happens, SUNDS stands for sudden unexplained nocturnal death syndrome. These men all died in their sleep."

"Were they cursed?" Father Rafael asked.

"Not exactly. Do you know what sleep paralysis is?"

"I do," Dr. Ashland volunteered. "I've experienced it twice. You wake up from a dead sleep unable to move. It feels as if someone's sitting on your chest, and you can just *sense* an evil, malevolent presence in the room. It's freaking terrifying. And I say that as someone who knows it's caused by an out-of-sync REM cycle." He shuddered at the memory.

"Right. Now, sleep paralysis is universal; it occurs in every known culture. But not every culture has a spiritual belief system that explains sleep paralysis as an evil spirit."

"Let me guess. The Hmong do," Father Rafael said.

"They do. And, in the case of the men who immigrated to the United States in the 1970s and 1980s, they didn't live in the equivalent of Chinatowns. They were spread out; they had no community. So they were unable to worship properly, and they believed this failure on their part angered the spirits."

"Which probably triggered a hormonal stress response, resulting in their deaths," Dr. Ashford surmised.

"So because the residents have been unable to perform the necessary Santerían rituals that will protect them from a death curse uttered by a powerful, vindictive *palero*, they're under psychological stress, which is peaking at night for some reason and killing them." Father Rafael summed it all up as though it was the most logical theory imaginable.

Bodhi relaxed back into his chair, a bit drained from having walked the group through the fruits of his overnight research frenzy in under ten minutes.

But his respite didn't last long.

"So what do we do about it?" Cleo demanded.

Bodhi smiled. "I'm glad you asked."

CHAPTER THIRTY-FIVE

Cleo smiled as warmly as she could manage at Philomena and Charlene. They looked back at her uncertainly.

"Thanks for coming in for a second day," she began. "I appreciate it so much."

"We heard about Mrs. Johnson's passing." Philomena bowed her head then clasped her hands together as if she were praying.

"It's so very sad. I wish the residents would accept the Lord into their hearts. Pastor Bryce can offer them more than just salvation, you know. Blessings abound if you believe." Charlene sounded genuinely pained at the thought that people were missing the riches boat.

"Yes. Well, I wanted to talk about something much more mundane. Some of the guests have reported that some personal items have gone missing. When I asked

Nurse Mumma about it, she told me that the cleaning procedures became much more stringent and detailed about a month ago. Right after Mr. Gonzales passed away."

"Yes, ma'am."

"I didn't change the procedures. So who did?"

"Oh, the instructions came from Pastor Bryce himself. He was appalled by the condition of Mr. Gonzales's room. Now, I know the guests are all adults, but Ms. Clarkson, if you'd seen it. Piles of dirt and rubbish everywhere. Two big metal pots just filled with trash of every imaginable kind. It was disgusting," Charlene remembered.

"Pastor Bryce saw it with his own eyes and just, well, he was beside himself," Philomena added.

"So what are your new procedures?"

"We haven't seen anything quite like Mr. Gonzales's room, thank the Lord. But we're to remove all fruit, flowers, and open food—like nuts or cake—that people leave out in the rooms. You know, before it can rot or decay." Philomena glanced at her friend, who nodded her agreement.

"Does that happen very often?"

"You'd be surprised," Charlene told her. "That and candles—which are also prohibited now. No open flames. That's just too dangerous."

"But for some reason, the Catholics are forever leaving food and dried herbs in front of their statues of the saints. And they fall asleep and leave candles burning!" Philomena was working herself into a state.

"Couldn't you just blow the candle out?" Cleo said as reasonably as she could.

"Oh, no. If they can't be trusted with using them safely, Pastor Bryce says they can't have them. Falling asleep with a lit candle, my goodness," Philomena countered.

"Hmm. Of course." Cleo studied the women. She considered herself a decent judge of character. They seemed to honestly believe they were simply keeping the guests safe and the rooms sanitary.

"Is there anything else, Ms. Clarkson?" Charlene's leg jiggled under the table.

Nervous. But why?

"What about wine? Did Pastor Bryce ask you to confiscate alcohol, too?"

Both women slowly shook their heads no. They wore twin expressions of confusion.

"Although I suppose if someone left a glass out, I'd dump it down the sink just like I'd dispose of the food," Philomena mused.

"Okay. Is there anything else Pastor Bryce asked either of you to do that I don't know about?"

Two sets of eyes dropped to the table. The room was completely silent.

Cleo let the silence hang long enough to become uncomfortable. Then, in a soft voice, she reminded them, "You work for me, not for him."

To her surprise, Charlene cracked before mousy Philomena did.

"There's one thing, but it's not related to my job here, it's related to the church ministry."

"And what's that, Charlene?" Cleo asked evenly.

"After Mr. Gonzales died, Pastor Bryce gave me this little doll and asked me to leave it on Mr. Ruiz's pillow when he wasn't in his room."

"A doll?" Cleo was sure she'd misheard. "Why?"

"He said that Mr. Gonzales and Mr. Ruiz had had a falling out, just before Mr. Gonzales died. You remember, the shoving match in the locker room?"

"Yes." The gossip mill had swung into high gear to spread that news. "But what's that have to do with a doll?"

"He said that when someone exchanges harsh words with a person right before they die, it can cause lingering guilt. And even though Mr. Ruiz wasn't a member of our church, the doll was a symbol of comfort to ease his mind." Charlene paused and twisted her lips. "I'll be honest, though, those little dolls are not well made. They're downright creepy, if you ask me. Anyway, he swore me to secrecy. I didn't even tell Philomena about it."

"Did you say *dolls* plural?"

"Yes. I did the same when Mr. Ruiz died. Pastor Bryce gave me a doll to leave for Mr. Caldron ..."

"Let me guess, when he died, you left a doll for Mr. Garcia, then one for Ms. Morales."

Charlene's eyes were enormous and her jaw was slack. She nodded mutely as she pieced together the pattern.

"But you weren't working last night," Cleo mused.

Charlene made a noise in her throat. "No, but he gave me the doll when we came in to meet with that lady detective. He said as long as Mrs. Johnson wasn't in her room, I was to leave it on her pillow right before I left the building. Otherwise, I should keep it until my next shift."

Cleo massaged her forehead. "What in the world—?"

"Ms. Clarkson?"

"Yes, Philomena."

"Pastor Bryce also swore me to secrecy about something." Her voice shook.

Cleo looked up. "What?"

"When Mr. Gonzales died, I found a big pile of

creepy little dolls in his bedside table. Pastor Bryce saw them and took them before I could put them in a box to take to the storage closet. He made me promise if I ever found another doll like that I would bring it straight to him and not tell a soul. So, that's what I did every time I cleaned out the room of someone who'd passed." She swallowed a sob and turned to Charlene. "That's why I always volunteered to clean the room after a passing."

"But you didn't work last night either."

"No, ma'am."

"Okay, thank you. Now, I'm sorry to be rude, but we're done here and I have something I have to do."

She rushed out of the conference room, already placing the call to Bodhi as she crossed the threshold. She didn't wait for him to speak.

As soon as he picked up, she said, "Pastor Scott knew. All of it. He's using their fear. I'm going to stay with my grandfather until this is over. You should tell Arthur to go to Mrs. Martin. I don't want them to be left alone."

She ended the call and raced down the hallway to the room where she knew she'd find her grandfather sitting by the window reading.

CHAPTER THIRTY-SIX

"You'll be fine," Felicia assured Arthur as she checked his wire and smoothed his jacket over the recording device taped to the small of his back.

In point of fact, she had zero confidence in his ability to pull this off. His knees were actually knocking together.

But even on the wafer-thin evidence Bodhi and Dr. Ashland had given her, she'd managed to convince Judge Young to sign off on a warrant, and she wasn't about to back out now. She simpered and preened and tossed her hair around like she was dancing for money to get the judge to approve her surveillance request. She sure as heck was going to surveil somebody.

As long as Arthur didn't pass out or puke, it shouldn't be too hard. He had one job: Get Scott to admit he was whipping up fear over the death cluster to incentivize the residents to join the Golden Island Church.

She gave him a light punch in the shoulder. "Go get 'em, kid."

Arthur gave her a sickly smile and started to walk, in slow motion, toward the cottage Pastor Scott used as his island office.

She positioned herself behind a large, flowering hibiscus plant. Then, reflexively, she made the sign of the cross.

Don't screw it up, Lopez.

A rthur forced himself to put one foot in front of the other. He'd always thought the saying was a cliche. But, as it turned out, it accurately described the process needed for him to make forward progress:

His brain issued the command *Move forward.*

His legs received the order and whimpered like cowards.

Finally, after a fierce argument over which one was going to do it, one of his legs would reluctantly raise its foot off the ground and inch forward.

Then its partner would wait for the brain to repeat the sequence.

Move forward.

He reminded himself why he was doing this. His *lita.* The woman who'd snuck him chocolate during the long, terrible eighth year of his childhood, when his parents had gone sugar-free. Who had taken him to see his first professional baseball game, where the Marlins had gotten the snot beaten out of them but she'd managed to snag a foul ball with her bare hand without spilling her beer.

He stopped at the door and leaned on the doorbell. He heard the chimes echoing inside the cottage.

After what seemed like a very long time, Pastor Bryce himself pulled the door open. Titanium-framed reading glasses were pushed up on his the top of his head.

"Arthur? What do you need? I'm working on my sermon for this weekend. I'm staying here specifically so I can write without interruption." He frowned.

"I'm ... sorry. I just really need some guidance."

Pastor Bryce sighed.

"It's my grandmother. She was ready to sign the check yesterday, but then her friend died. Now she's a wreck, and I can't seem to get her to focus. I thought maybe you could give me some pointers, so I can be a closer." Arthur worried that he was rambling.

Pastor Bryce looked past him, out into the garden.

For an interminable moment, Arthur thought the pastor had spotted Detective Williams.

It's all over.

His heart tightened in his chest. He tried to swallow, but the lump in his throat was a boulder.

He made a noise that sounded shamefully like a whimper.

But then a light sparked in Pastor Bryce's eyes, and he smiled. He placed a strong hand on Arthur's shoulder and squeezed it.

"Arthur, son, I'm going to tell you exactly what to do. Follow my instructions to a tee, and your grandmother will be begging to write that check." He laughed.

"Uh ... great."

"Listen, carefully. Your grandmother *should* be scared. Her friends are dying. *Dying.* And the reason why they're dying is the Lord is angry with them. Tell her Father Rafael can't protect her from His vengeance. But *I* can. *You* can. Tell her if she makes an offering to the Lord of your buy-in fee and joins Golden Shores with a prorated annual tithing payment, *she will be protected.* Then, ask her to pray with you."

Pastor Bryce reached into his pocket and found the doll he'd removed from Lynette Johnson's pillow the night before. He pressed it into Arthur's hand. "Hold her hand in prayer, and while her eyes are closed, place this doll on her pillow. Don't mention it. Don't point it out. Just wait and trust."

Arthur stared down at the clothespin. A crude face was painted on the wooden head. Black fuzz served as hair. A scrap of fabric was glued on as clothing. And a black heart was drawn on the doll's chest.

"What is it?"

Pastor Bryce laughed again. "It's better than a blue chip stock. It's mortal fear."

Arthur blinked at him.

"Now, go over to Golden Shores and do what I said. I need to get back to work. But tomorrow, I know we will be celebrating your success and praising the Lord."

Pastor Bryce stepped back into his hallway and shut the door in Arthur's face.

He stood, dejected, on the porch for several seconds then slumped his way back to the garden where Detective Williams was waiting for him.

"I'm so sorry," he moaned as she reached up his

shirt to stop the recording and remove the device. "I blew it. He wouldn't even let me in the house. And he gave me this stupid doll."

She punched him in the arm again. "Wrong-o, Arthur. That stupid doll nails him to the wall. You did it!"

She smiled broadly.

He stared at her, startled by the transformation in her whole demeanor from hardened to happy.

"I did?"

CHAPTER THIRTY-SEVEN

Cleo and Mr. Santiago were playing chess when Father Rafael and Mrs. Martin appeared in the doorway to his room. The priest wore a white shirt. He looked unfamiliar without his head-to-toe black and clerical collar.

"We need you to join us in the social club's meeting room," Father Rafael said in a grave voice.

Cleo felt her eyes widen. "Is everyone okay?"

"We will be. Detective Williams called and said it's 'go time.' I presume that means those of us seeking protection should take the necessary steps." He patted the satchel at his side.

Mr. Santiago's eyes darted toward Cleo. "Maybe not right now, Father."

Mrs. Martin shook her head. "It's okay, Hector. Father Rafael says she knows."

"It's true," Cleo assured him.

A s Mr. Santiago and Mrs. Martin prepared the altar to Saint Theresa, who also represented Oyá, the orisha who guarded the gateway between Life and Death, Father Rafael kept up a running commentary.

Cleo assumed it was for her benefit.

"Because the *palero* Gonzales has cursed Julia and Hector with death, they will make offerings to Oyá, seeking her protection from Death. She will make sure they don't pass her threshold too soon."

He reached into his pouch and pulled out several beaded bracelets, which he passed around.

"Oyá's favorite colors are burgundy and brown. Wear the bracelet on your left wrist," he told Cleo as she started to fasten it around her right.

She quickly switched it to the other wrist.

Next from the satchel, came a bag of plums and a container of chocolate pudding.

"Oyá likes sweet dark foods and red wines." He nodded to Mrs. Martin, who took a bottle of wine and a corkscrew from her purse.

"Is that Lynette's missing wine?" Cleo asked.

"Well, it's one of them." Mrs. Martin winked. "She went out special to get them so we could make an offering to Oyá. Then, when she died, I just knew the bottles would vanish, so I took them first. When her niece told you they'd gone missing, I just chimed in and made a big production about my missing candle."

"Misdirection," Hector Santiago said in a deadpan voice. "Very nice."

Father Rafael cleared his throat. "Before we start and I assume the role of your *santero*, there's something I need to say as your priest."

Mrs. Martin and Mr. Santiago stopped kidding around and stood up straighter.

"It's important that, when you pray to a saint or to God or otherwise, you *believe*. It's not the offering or the prayer that will protect you from the *palero's* curse. It's your belief that you have done the things you must do to protect yourself." Father Rafael paused and searched their faces. "Terrible things have happened in this place, but you're being protected now. And I believe you will be safe here from now on. But you must believe it, too."

"Yes, Father," Mrs. Martin whispered.

"Yes, Father."

"Okay, then let's get started."

"Do you have a black hen in that purse of yours?" Mr. Santiago asked.

"No blood sacrifice today, Hector. Oyá's powerful enough in this situation that we don't need an animal. And this is a man sack, thank you very much." He patted his bag.

Cleo focused on slowing her rapid heartbeat.

CHAPTER THIRTY-EIGHT

Three things shine before the world and cannot be hidden. They are the moon, the sun, and the truth[.]

POKALA LAKSHMI NARASU,
THE ESSENCE OF BUDDHISM
(1907)

For nothing is secret that will not be revealed, nor anything hidden that will not be known and come to light.

LUKE 8:17

Bodhi leaned against the cool glass that fronted Golden Shores' lobby and watched as Arthur Lopez followed Detective Williams careful instructions.

He squeaked into his cell phone, "Pastor Bryce, she's dead. My grandmother. Can you come to the building? Please hurry."

A pause. Arthur caught Bodhi's eye and gave him a thumb's up sign.

"What? The doll. Yes, I think I can pocket it before anyone sees."

Another pause.

"Okay, yes. Please, hurry."

He ended the call and gave Detective Williams a beseeching look. "Am I done?"

"You're done. Go ahead inside. I think your grandmother's in the library with Father Rafael."

She smiled at Bodhi as Arthur ran into the building before she could change her mind. "I had my doubts about him, but he's pretty solid."

"So, what's the plan now?"

She patted her side. "I have my service weapon and a set of cuffs. The plan is pretty straightforward." She glanced in his direction again. "But you might want to make yourself scarce. You're banned from the building, remember?"

Bodhi looked to his left then to his right. "I don't seem to be *in* the building. Besides what if you need backup?"

Detective Williams giggled. "What're you gonna do if I do? Meditate at him?"

It was a fair point, he had to admit. Even Bodhi wouldn't choose himself to have his back in a physical altercation.

She grew more serious. "If this is misplaced machismo, you can save it. I can take care of myself."

He was certain she could. "No, that's not it. I think I just ... I want the closure of seeing him arrested for terrorizing these people. Can you imagine being so scared that you died? That's a horrifying thought."

His answer surprised him. He was well-known among friends for urging forgiveness, yet here he was seeking something that sounded and felt an awful lot like vengeance. That was a dark impulse.

Before he could investigate it further, Bryce Scott came jogging into view.

"Detective," he called, "I've heard about Mrs. Martin."

"It's so strange—Ed's not working, yet here we are

with another dead person in your assisted living facility," Detective Williams remarked coolly.

Pastor Scott blinked. "Yes, well—" He must have noticed Bodhi in his peripheral vision because he made a choking noise. "Get off my island. Joel Ashland may be useless, but you're worse than useless. You've brought nothing but chaos to Golden Shores. Ms. Clarkson is questioning my leadership, the employees are being harassed by the police, and people continue to die."

Bodhi smiled placidly.

The pastor blustered, "Detective, I demand you arrest this man for trespassing."

Detective Williams nodded. "I can make an arrest."

"Good."

She reached into her trouser pocket. Instead of taking out her handcuffs, she removed the Palo mayombe doll. With a fast motion, she fired it at Scott like a baseball pitcher.

He reached out reflexively and caught the item hurtling toward him. When he held it to his face to see what it was, he stammered, "How did you ... where?"

Detective Williams stepped forward with her handcuffs ready. "Bryce Scott, you're under arrest—"

As she recited the pastor's rights to him, Bodhi

turned away and settled his gaze on the cerulean water. Whether Bryce Scott ultimately went to prison for his actions was out of Bodhi's hands. But he could ensure that the people in Golden Shores were protected and well.

He closed his eyes. It seemed like as good a time as any for a quick *metta bhavana* practice.

CHAPTER THIRTY-NINE

A rthur hugged his grandmother tightly. She rubbed his back. After a long while, he pulled back and held her at arm's length.

"I'm so sorry you've had to go through this ... hell, *lita.* I'm going to get you out of here. You'll come live with me."

She patted his cheek. "Oh, Arturo, you're so sweet."

"I was wrong about Pastor Scott."

Her clear brown eyes burned into his. "Yes, you were. But then you were brave and strong. But I don't want to live with you. My home is here." She waved a hand.

"But—"

"No, *nieto,* I want to stay. My friends are here." She opened her purse and took out her checkbook.

"*Lita*, you don't need to give me any money. I'm not buying into the ministry. I'm leaving the church."

She ignored him, wrote her careful signature on a blank check, then tore it from the register, and handed it to him. "You listen to me, Arturo. You're smart. You start a business. A real business, not some pyramid scheme or scam to separate Christians from their money. This is about what you can offer the world. Pray on it. And when you know, fill in the amount for how much you need. Plus ten dollars."

Arthur grasped the check tightly, as if to reassure himself that it was real. "Plus ten?"

"You're going to need a new San Sebastian candle for a new venture. And make sure—"

"I'll be sure to get the oil and the herbs, *lita*."

She laughed, and her whole face lit up. "I love you, Arturo."

He pulled her in for another hug.

On the other side of the meeting room, Cleo was helping Mr. Santiago clean up the altar to Oyá. She glanced over at Arthur and Mrs. Martin, hugging, and her heart swelled.

She blinked back tears and turned to Mr. Santiago.

Then she turned the red and brown beads on the bracelet Father Rafael had placed on her wrist.

Worrying them, she heard Lynette's voice say in her head.

She made a noise that was half-laugh/half-sob.

Mr. Santiago looked up from the pudding and wine in front of the Saint Theresa statue with concern. "Cleo, are you okay? Your first ritual can be an emotional experience. Maybe sit down?"

She shook her head. "I'm fine."

"What is past is left behind. The future is as yet unreached." Bodhi's words echoed in her mind.

Her grandfather turned his attention back to the altar.

"Mr. Santiago?"

"Yes?"

She exhaled. "I have something I need to tell you."

CHAPTER FORTY

After watching one final Sugarloaf Key sunrise over the water, Bodhi washed his bowl and mug from breakfast at the small sink in the camper's kitchenette. He was drying them when a silver coupe came into view through the window. He placed the bowl and mug on the shelf where he'd found them then hung the dish towel over the metal bar affixed to the wall.

He walked outside and shielded his eyes against the morning sun as Cleo switched off the engine and stepped out of the car.

"Good morning. If you're looking for Joel, I'm sorry to say you've missed him. He and Detective Williams had an early morning meeting with the county commissioners about Bryce Scott."

"I know. I'm scheduled to meet with them myself in an hour. But I'm here to see you."

She swallowed, and he could see her throat move.

"Oh."

She moved around the car to come stand beside him. She was close enough that he could smell her shampoo when the breeze lifted her hair off her shoulders.

"I hear you're leaving today."

He nodded. "Yes. Father Rafael and I had our meetings with the politicians yesterday. So, there's no reason for me to stick around."

Her green eyes were wide and clear, but her quick, shallow breathing betrayed her nerves.

"Sure."

"I think Golden Shores is going to come out of this fine, Cleo—"

"I think so, too. The plan I've heard being bandied around is that I'll continue to run the facility with state oversight. And, of course, with a promise not to favor *any* religion over another. I'm really not sure how I'll manage any requests to perform animal sacrifices, though." She shook her head at the thought.

"What about Pastor Scott?"

She raised her slight shoulders in a 'who knows' gesture. "Lynette's niece thinks he'll be charged with negligent homicide, at a minimum. He's already started a special collection at the church for his legal fees."

"So ..." he trailed off, unsure why she was there and unwilling to make any assumptions.

"So. I wanted to let you know I told Mr. Santiago that I'm his granddaughter." She let out a long, shaky breath.

"That's great. Really. No matter how he took it, it was the right step for you. How *did* he take it?"

Her full lips quirked up in a smile. "He's thrilled. Kind of giddy, actually. Of course, so am I. We have a pickleball date tonight before dinner."

Her joy was contagious. "Fantastic."

"Yeah, so anyway. I just wanted to thank you for pushing me to do it."

She darted toward him and kissed his cheek. She had already pulled away by the time he registered the gesture. She hopped into her car and waved goodbye.

As he watched her pull away, Detective Williams pulled up with Dr. Ashland in her passenger seat. The two women greeted one other with short beeps of their horns while Dr. Ashland gave Bodhi an exaggerated thumbs up through the car window.

Over Bodhi's protests that he could call a cab, Joel Ashland and Felicia Williams insisted on driving him to the airport.

On the one hand, it gave him a chance to say goodbye to two colleagues who'd become friends. On the other hand, it meant another white-knuckled trip barreling down the Overseas Highway with Detective Williams at the wheel.

Detective Williams parked the sedan in the same no-parking zone she'd violated when she'd picked him up. She turned on her flashers and popped the trunk.

Bodhi grabbed his bag and turned to shake her hand. "It was a pleasure working with you, Detective Williams."

She shook her head. "Come on, now. We're in Key West. You can call me Felicia." She pulled his hand toward her and caught him in a quick embrace.

"Goodbye, Felicia."

"Goodbye, Bodhi. Thanks for the anger management tips." She laughed.

"You should laugh more, Felicia. It's a beautiful sound."

She blushed. Dr. Ashland came around to the back of the car to shake Bodhi's hand.

"Thanks for helping out, Bodhi. You saved my

bacon. And Eduardo Martinez's. Let me know if I can ever return the favor."

"I will. Thanks for putting me up in the camper."

"Don't mention it." Dr. Ashland gave him a solid pat on the back.

The three of them looked at one another for a long moment. After being together in the crucible of the investigation, it seemed strange to be going separate ways.

"Well."

"Yes."

Bodhi shouldered his duffle bag. "Please keep me posted on any developments at Golden Shores."

As he walked away, Dr. Ashland called, "I'm sure Cleo would be happy to stay in touch."

He shook his head but just kept walking.

He had to smile, though, when Felicia Williams's silvery, bell-like laugh caught the wind.

He stepped into the terminal without looking back.

CHAPTER FORTY-ONE

Several weeks later

Bodhi was raking fallen leaves at the monastery. The weak autumn sun warmed his shoulders. The crisp air filled his lungs. He moved rhythmically, the motion of his arms and the intake of his breath in tandem.

The dry and crackling leaves were mostly shades of brown. As he shaped them into a tidy pile, glints of red, yellow, and orange winked up at him. He smiled down at them.

Daishin crossed the lawn. "Are you well?"

He considered the question. Yes, he was very well. "I am."

"You seem it." The novice monk watched him

work the rake for a moment. "No decisions intruding on your peace now?"

He shook his head. "Not now."

"What will you do?"

"Rake."

Daishin rewarded him with a half-smile. "Raking is good. And then?"

Bodhi stopped and leaned against the implement. "I like the quiet. But if I'm called to help, I will."

"So, you plan to offer your services as an independent forensic pathology consultant, then?"

Daishin's insight startled him for a moment—until he remembered that before taking up his robes, the monk had earned his MBA.

"As a matter of fact, that is the plan."

Daishin nodded. "It's a good plan."

They regarded the mound of leaves together. Bodhi scanned the lawn for stray leaves but saw none.

"I think I'm finished here."

Another nod from Daishin.

He said his goodbyes to the monk and began the short walk home.

When he was a third of the way to his house, his cell phone vibrated in his pocket. He stopped at a bus shelter to sit and answer it.

"Hello?"

"*Bon jour*. I am trying to reach a Dr. Bodhi King." A polished voice with an accent he placed as French-Canadian, the voice of a stranger, sounded in his ear.

"This is Bodhi."

"Dr. King, my name is Guillaume Loomis. I'm coordinating the programming for the upcoming meeting of the North American Society of Forensic Pathology, which will take place here in Québec City later this year."

"Yes?"

"You've submitted a paper to our journal, I believe?"

He had. He'd been inspired to begin writing it on the plane back from Key West and had sent it out as soon he and Dr. Ashland had agreed that it was fit for publication.

"That's right. The working title is 'Scared to Death: When Beliefs Kill.'"

"Yes, that's the one. I'm calling to tell you that we've accepted it for publication in the symposium issue that will coincide with the conference."

"Great. Thanks for the call."

"We also want to invite you to present your findings at the meeting."

Bodhi felt his jaw hinge open. "Oh? I'm honored, of course. But Joel Ashland, my coauthor, might be a better choice. Dr. Ashland's the medical examiner for the county where the death cluster discussed in the paper occurred."

"Yes," Guillaume said patiently. "I'm aware of his position. We're interested in your perspective, as a pathologist who has now handled two disparate SUD clusters, Dr. King. The panel we'd like you to sit on is 'Forensic Black Swans—When the Pathologist Confronts the Unimaginable.'"

The topic intrigued him. "It does sound interesting."

"I'm confident that it will be worth your time, Dr. King. We're assembling a truly unique panel. And, if you've never been to our city, it's breathtaking."

Bodhi reflected for a heartbeat. "I'd love to present."

"Ah, *fantastique*. If you can provide your assistant's contact information, I'll confirm that your schedule will permit you to join us and will forward all the pertinent information."

"I don't have an assistant."

There was an awkward silence.

"Oh, but of course. Well, let me just give you the dates, and you can see if they'll work, yes?"

"My calendar's clear, Dr. Loomis. I'm sure I'm available."

"I see. Then I'll just send the packet to the email address given in your article."

"Wonderful. Have a peaceful day."

"I will? Er, I will. You as well."

"Oh, I will," Bodhi assured him.

He ended the call and leaned against the back of the bench. He pocketed the phone then turned his face toward the sky and inhaled deeply.

THANK YOU!

Bodhi will be back in his next adventure soon! If you enjoyed this book, I'd love it if you'd help introduce others to the series.

Share it. Please lend your copy to a friend.

Review it. Consider posting a short review to help other readers decide whether they might enjoy it.

Connect with me. Stop by my Facebook page for book updates, cover reveals, pithy quotes about coffee, and general time-wasting.

Sign up. To be the first to know when I have a new release, sign up for my email newsletter at www.melissafmiller.com. I only send emails when I have book news—I promise.

While I'm busy writing the next book, if you haven't read my Sasha McCandless, my Aroostine

Higgins series, or my We Sisters Three series, you might want to give them a try.

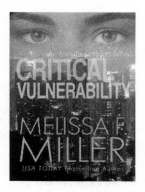

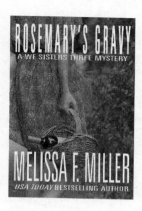

ABOUT THE AUTHOR

USA Today bestselling author Melissa F. Miller was born in Pittsburgh, Pennsylvania. Although life and love led her to Philadelphia, Baltimore, Washington, D.C., and, ultimately, South Central Pennsylvania, she secretly still considers Pittsburgh home.

In college, she majored in English literature with concentrations in creative writing poetry and medieval literature and was STUNNED, upon graduation, to learn that there's not exactly a job market for such a degree. After working as an editor for several years, she returned to school to earn a law degree. She was that annoying girl who loved class and always raised her hand. She practiced law for fifteen years, including a stint as a clerk for a federal judge, nearly a decade as an attorney at major international law firms, and several years running a two-person law firm with her lawyer husband.

Now, powered by coffee, she writes legal thrillers and homeschools her three children. When she's not writing, and sometimes when she is, Melissa travels around the country in an RV with her husband, her kids, and her cat.

Connect with me:

www.melissafmiller.com

ACKNOWLEDGMENTS

Many thanks to everyone involved in the production of this book—in particular, my phenomenal editing and design team.

32044142R00212

Made in the USA
Lexington, KY
27 February 2019